SAVING WOMEN

SAVING WOMEN

A Collection of Short Stories

FRANK DEWEY STALEY

SAVING WOMEN
A COLLECTION OF SHORT STORIES

iUniverse books may be ordered through booksellers or by contacting:

iUniverse
1663 Liberty Drive
Bloomington, IN 47403
www.iuniverse.com
844-349-9409

Because of the dynamic nature of the Internet, any web addresses or links contained in this book may have changed since publication and may no longer be valid. The views expressed in this work are solely those of the author and do not necessarily reflect the views of the publisher, and the publisher hereby disclaims any responsibility for them.

Any people depicted in stock imagery provided by Getty Images are models, and such images are being used for illustrative purposes only.
Certain stock imagery © Getty Images.

ISBN: 978-1-6632-1840-7 (sc)
ISBN: 978-1-6632-1841-4 (e)

Library of Congress Control Number: 2021902673

Print information available on the last page.

iUniverse rev. date: 02/09/2021

Dedication

To Geraldine Flynn Staley, the original Saving Woman

CONTENTS

NEW MEXICO

I WAS HAVING A DIFFICULT TIME reminding myself that my father had died. He visited my office a few days ago and took me out for a dinner of steamed crabs. As usual, he ordered a brilliant wine…a really crisp Sauvignon Blanc from New Zealand; we drank two bottles.

"You picking up that hint of citrus?" he asked.

I had picked up something… you could not grow up his daughter and not anticipate something nice from a glass of wine he had selected… but had been unable to identify the subtlety until he mentioned it.

"For sure," I said.

And now I had to remind myself that he was gone. So I had learned, on his way back to his new place in New Mexico, his single engine airplane had gone down. Not a fearless pilot by any means… he flew airplanes like he had conducted most of the affairs of his life; cautious and somewhat calculating, he retained the ability to know when it was time to leap.

"We all have opportunities to cross the Rubicon," he used to say, "but very few of us do."

So here I was sitting alone in my office reminding myself that he was gone. My father. My dad. Those blue eyes, those strong hands, the shoulders, were all gone now. I did not expect to have to deal with these feelings for years.

He had done well financially, if not romantically. Two ex-wives, the first being my mother, a horrifically devastating relationship with a lesbian woman (he was the last to know), and a brief spell of pointless and fruitless dating all added up to solitude in his last months. In his late fifties, my father knew all the moves, but did not approve of many.

Only this year, exactly three months ago, he had gone into

semi-retirement and settled on a small horse ranch in New Mexico. He and my stepmother had honeymooned there, and dad was instantly taken with the high skies, the paint-by-number sunsets and the warmth of the people. It was a genuine artist community, Taos, and dad had purchased a three or four acre patch of scrubland on the outskirts of town. He had e-mailed me pictures of the small ranch house as it went through its refurbishment. The trees were spindly, but the mountains in the background were breathtaking. We hadn't, my sisters and I, had a chance to visit.

It was a job now, grieving for my father. There was work to do. His "affairs" had to be settled. My understanding was that the homestead he had selected in New Mexico would have to be visited. Paintings and pictures, all of those fragments of our years together and apart, would have to be boxed up and distributed. It was a job, but a job with a road map.

John Kvaros was dad's lawyer and confident for as long as I could remember. Dad, evidently, had left some pretty detailed orders for John in the event of his death. John, ever the friend and servant, followed them to the letter.

He phoned me on a Friday and asked if he and I could spend some of the next day together. I hadn't seen him since he and dad surprised me in Elmira, New York the summer I turned twenty and was finding myself as an actress.

"The best chorus dancer I've ever seen," John had told me over drinks and dinner after the Sunday matinee.

So here he was outside my apartment door promptly at noon. He carried a leather lawyer's case stuffed, I was to find out, with three of dad's journals, assorted pictures and pounds of letters.

My father spoke often of John, always in appreciation and awe. John was perhaps the only openly gay man in our tiny hometown, and dad felt both sympathy for his aloneness as well as admiration for his ability to deal with small-town homophobic bullshit. John always took our calls when my sisters and I phoned, and his advice was on the money every time.

"Hello, Lauren. I'm so sorry that we have to see each other after all this time under such a heavy cloud."

He winked at me as a reflex before engulfing me in his long lawyer arms. His cream-colored sweater smelled like ocean air as he hugged me.

We made tea...Irish Breakfast Tea in tribute to my father...and sat on the floor of my tiny living room. John seemed comfortable in his jeans and sweater. He was one of the last true suit and tie men, but had flown in comfort to D.C. that morning to see me.

"Before we get going, I need to tell you that some of what we're going to see and discuss is going to come as a surprise to you. I'm also charged with sending you on a journey. Your father has made it clear that you are to do him a favor. You ready?"

And so I learned about my father's secret. Had she been just another woman, with all that casual phrase conjures up, it would have been a breeze. Lots and lots of men have other women. Very few of them are close relatives.

"From what your father told me over the years, and from what I can glean from what's in my bag here, their relationship was never consummated," said John. "I don't know if that was out of some sense of decorum on your father's part, or if he simply felt it was a complication the two of them should not be forced to deal with."

And so we sat on the carpeted floor and poured over the pictures, letters, journals, the occasional birthday or get-well-soon card. My father and his cousin: Joe and Layla.

It felt intrusive to be reading these things. Dad was not gone in my mind. I could still taste citrus. But John kept me going with frequent urgings that dad had arranged all of this. Dad had requested that I be filled in. It was important to him that I obtain a real sense of the degree of love...friendship...longing, whatever we choose to call whatever it was that existed between the two of them. It was real. That was obvious from the first letter I read. In every photo we looked at, the two of them seemed purposely positioned away from one another. What handsome and charismatic people they were. I cried at the thought of their solitude, suffered while so close to what they probably pined for.

After reading every word of what John had brought along, I marveled that dad could have kept this all so private for such a long time. Of course we'd all met Layla, knew her children, kept up via holiday cards and such. But none of us, not one of us would have dreamed that she and dad could have maintained such an intense and consuming relationship for so long a time. The sexual tension must have been electric.

"So what's the mission?" I asked.

John and I had finished our work getting up to speed on the secret history and had walked the three blocks to an upscale little café I visited often. We were eating baked lasagna and drinking a bottle of Chianti. Dad loved Italian food and the wide variety of wines that could be consumed with it.

"He wants...he wanted you to visit Layla and take her to his home in New Mexico. There are things he wanted her to have, and I think he anticipated that you could guide her through the emotional storm, so to speak."

John had pushed the sleeves of his sweater up to his elbows and had folded his giant hands as if in prayer. He looked at me as if I were about to be cross-examined.

"When?" I asked. "Where does Layla live now?"

"As soon as you can work it out," said John. "Layla lives in Wisconsin. I'll leave her contact information with you; just let me know of the expenses you incur, and I'll get you reimbursed promptly. I think it's very important that this little trip happen as soon as possible. Layla may be reluctant to go, but I have faith...your father had faith in your ability to convince her."

I enjoyed a kaleidoscopic video trailer in my head for a moment chronicling many of the thoughtful things my father had done for me: teaching me to swim, talking me through boyfriend problems, hitting tennis ball after tennis ball until my strokes were sound, dragging me to concerts I knew I would hate but quickly loved.

"I'll leave tomorrow," I said. "I love surprising people."

I flew to Milwaukee the next morning and rented a car for the two hour trip north. Layla had not moved from the house she and her ex-husband had built just west of Green Bay. They had divorced years ago, and I wondered what kind of heavy and exhausting baggage she and dad had carried as a result of the life-long affections each maintained for the other. No wonder their marriages crumbled.

The drive north gave me some time to rehearse my lines. How could she not agree? It also gave me time to chronicle my own life a bit. Never married, no children, focused on nothing but work. I seemed to bounce from one job to another, a career lifestyle dad warned me about. Maybe this trip was his way to engage me from the alleged afterworld, to encourage me to stick to the course, any course, a bit longer. Maybe Layla was in on the ruse.

I pulled into the drive of her modest and neat home. A green pickup truck was parked in the drive; the tailgate was down.

I should have called, but knew that news of someone's death, particularly when the someone had been the object of Layla's affection for so long, should be delivered in person.

She was as I remembered and what the photos of the previous day had refocused: tall, fit, dressed in jeans, sweatshirt and boots; she could have been a model. She smiled an instant before recognizing me, a development that gave me a glimpse into one of the characteristics my father must have loved: Layla wanted to like people.

"Layla, I'm Lauren. Joe's daughter."

Her smile now full, Layla stepped off the porch and walked purposefully toward me extending her arms more with each step.

"Oh my God, you have grown up into such a beautiful woman. Your pictures simply don't do you justice."

"Thank you, Layla. I hope you don't mind me coming by unannounced."

By now she had put her arms around me and was holding on. She felt thin, but womanly; delicate, but firm. I would not have been surprised to learn that she had just hefted several fifty pound bags of pottery clay from her truck to the work shed behind the house.

"I'm afraid I have some bad news for you."

I would have preferred to stay in the clinches with her at the moment she discovered my father was dead. I did not want to have the countenance of her face, her expression of fear and loss, burned into my memory for even an instant. But that was not Layla. Hers was more a head on style of approaching life. She stepped away and continued to hold my hands. Her eyes were blue; her bottom lip, almost imperceptibly, trembled.

"What is it?" she asked.

"It's my father. He's died in a plane crash."

We do what we can to lighten the load placed on our shoulders from minute to minute, day to day. Layla, in love with a man she could not touch for her entire adult life probably knew more about this concept than any of us. But the weight of this news clearly punished her. She seemed in an instant to lose inches from her height.

She exhaled loudly as her eyes filled with tears. She released my hands and ran her fingers through her hair. I was almost disappointed not to be able to achieve the same depth of sorrow.

"Come in," she said. "I assume there's a reason I'm learning this in person."

The next two days were a combination of catharsis and confrontation. Layla shared her secrets with me; I began to deal with the fact that my life was no less unfulfilled than hers had been. My father, the great thinker, seemed to know exactly what he was doing by putting us together.

We drank lots of cold beer and expensive wine, ate high end meals at the best restaurants we could find, and became, almost instantly, great, great friends. We shared the love of our losing; our conversations ran from teary whispers to loud and long laughter.

"Your father and I enjoyed the game of flirting with each other from really early on," said Layla. We were sitting at her kitchen table sipping ice cold cinnamon schnapps. It was extremely late. "We both had been approached by members of our families wanting to know if we were sleeping together, so we made it a point to keep as much distance between us as possible. But we wrote steamy letters, we had lots of juicy phone calls… It was great fun despite the frustration."

"Did you ever think about acting on it? I mean, you were both adults, your kids were grown. Why not?"

"He asked and I said no. Or I would bring it up and he wasn't ready at the moment. Eventually, we sort of settled into what we had. If what I felt for your father, what I *feel* for him is love, then I have never been in love with anyone else."

Layla had impressed me throughout our hours together with her strength and willingness to share intimate and warming details of her relationship with my father. I was overwhelmed with sadness that they had been so close to realizing genuine love and affection, but had never been able to take the step.

"Layla," I said, this time taking her hands into mine, "I have to go to New Mexico. There are things I have to attend to at dad's place. I want you to go with me."

When we are filled with sorrow and cannot imagine ourselves capable of even one more ounce of pain, we sometimes look for it. Layla nodded and smiled.

"I've never been to New Mexico," she said.

The next day, a brilliant and beautiful fall sunrise brightened Layla and I as we headed to the airport. We listened to the radio and spoke very little. We had both said so much over the last two days, it seemed almost necessary to sit through a few miles of silence. There was also the visit to dad's ranch looming on the western horizon.

I reread another of the journals John had presented me as Layla slept in her window seat. Strikingly pretty with high cheek bones and a delicate jaw, her lips were slightly parted as she slept. An almost imperceptible tracing of saliva had formed at the corner of her mouth.

"I wait for you like a dog," he had written

"I have thought about sex with you, and I have been driven to moments of madness."

"L told me today, in no uncertain terms or waffling, that she loved me. My spirit soared."

"L closed her letter to me today by calling me 'her pearl.' My heart leapt miles into space."

I woke at touchdown and figured I deserved the crick in my neck; journals written by one's father should perhaps not be explored.

Neither of us anticipated the strange beauty of the high desert, the mountains, the adobe architecture, to grab us up so quickly.

"No wonder he settled out here," said Layla. "He talked about it all the time, he asked me a hundred times to meet him out here."

"Why didn't you?" I asked.

"The time just never seemed right," she trailed off.

We drove on in pleasant silence, the magnificence of the countryside offset by the anxiety we both were surely feeling.

At Taos, we stopped for bottles of water at a roadside store. The men inside spoke in a Native American language and seemed not to notice us. The shopkeeper was friendly and gave us our final directions to the road on which dad's ranch sat.

"Well, "I said as I started the car, "I guess it's crunch time."

Four miles at sixty miles per hour does not equate to four minutes. Neither are we able, not ever, to precisely predict the outcome of a journey regardless of how well we practice the steps we anticipate taking along its way.

I pulled into the driveway and stopped; the fifty yards or so from the road to the house lay before us. The mountains in the background to the west had begun to glow as the sun rested at their tops for final moments before diving down to the Pacific Ocean. Birds chirped, but the only sounds available to either of us were heartbeats.

I looked closely at Layla. It was the appointed hour. I saw in her reaction the man step out of the house onto the porch; I saw fear, hope, a tracing of anger, relief, eagerness, the end of the loneliness, and...yes, there it was...love.

"Time to cross the Rubicon, Layla."

I smiled for the first time in my life.

THE SUGAR ISLAND ARTIST COMMUNITY

MARTIN

T HE LAST TIME I SAW Martin Stewart was when he had relentlessly stalked my niece Bitsy.

My best friend through college, Martin had asked her to marry while attending one of my family's reunions. In a moment of insanity exclusive to the human sexuality love dynamic, she said yes.

Young, extremely attractive and talented, she had confused what I'm sure was a deep-seated longing for a father figure with whatever the hell it was that Martin was throwing her way. He was not a bad guy. He carried with him an intensity that did not appeal to all appetites, but he could also be charming, supportive and loyal.

She called me from her apartment in California on a Tuesday night.

"Unc, I need to talk to you, and I'm afraid that what I'm going to tell you might make you mad or disappointed."

Conversation starters such as this never fail to grab the listener's attention.

"You need some money, Bits?"

"No, it's about Martin. Your friend Martin."

"You don't have to marry him, sweetie."

"How did you know?"

That's one of the often charming endearments of young people, especially young people related to us: they attribute wisdom to acts of recollection or logical conclusion.

"I thought your relationship with my friend Martin was destined to die a rather quick death. I'm surprised, to be honest, that it's taken this long for you to arrive at this decision."

"He's a really nice guy, Unc, but the age thing, and he's so locked into every little thing."

"You don't need to explain. Listen, have you talked to him yet?"

"I'm calling him as soon as I get off the phone with you,"

"Good luck and let me know if you need any help from me."

Martin lived a few hundred miles down the coast from his soon-to-be-ex-fiancée, so it made sense that Bitsy end the relationship with a phone call. Martin apparently failed to see the logic of her decision. He bugged her for two weeks before she felt it necessary to call me again.

"I don't want to call the police, Unc, but he's relentless. He's in town now all the time."

"Don't call the police," I said. "I'll handle this."

"It's just that he calls me incessantly. He comes to my work. Last night I was leaving the gym with a girlfriend and he was parked next to me."

"Did he say anything?"

"He told me that I was one of God's perfect little creatures, or some such shit, and that he wanted to get coffee."

"I got this," I said.

We met in high school and attended the same college for our first two years. Martin was a tall, thin guy with black hair. He tended more towards dark clothing and always had a backpack slung over his shoulder. We shared a love of reading, and both fancied ourselves to be writers.

Less realistic than I, Martin was consumed by romance. It was all about the moments for him: the look on the face of a woman awkwardly receiving a gift he'd picked out for her; some girl casually brushing the hair out of her face; the manner in which this woman or that chewed her pizza. He even developed an odd anticipation for the instant each of these women invariably asked him to leave them alone.

"It was a wonderful moment," he would tell me. "My heart is broken, it truly is, Conor. I'll go to my grave believing that she was the one. But she looked so innocently beautiful telling me to fuck off. I'll never lose that image."

He hinted once about an uncomfortable experience he'd gone through as a kid, and I'm sure whatever that was influenced his capability to act within conventional parameters with the opposite sex. But this was the tail end of the sexual revolution in America. And despite whatever coaching assistance I offered, he never was able to swim in the mainstream. I don't believe he had sex once in the two years we were at school together. If he did, he did not tell me about it, and that would have been highly unusual.

He turned out to be a perfect companion from a literary standpoint. We each wrote several stories and a raft of poems, spent hours analyzing them, and then made a game of collecting rejection slips from some of the more prestigious magazines and journals in the country. At night, we would sit in the pub, drinking draft beers and taking ourselves way too seriously.

Occasionally, Martin would laser lock on some artsy and earthy girl, invite her to join us, and then watch stoically as I left with her. I always clandestinely received his approval before acting. He did not live vicariously through these encounters. He never asked for details and he always forgave me.

So here I was exiting a cab and striding up the walk to Martin's house in California. This was a conversation I had pointedly decided to have in person.

"What the hell are you doing here?" he asked. "It's great to see you, Conor. Come in. Come in."

We took seats facing each other from across his kitchen table. He offered to make coffee, but I wanted to wait and see how the conversation went before accepting.

"To what do I owe the pleasure?" he asked.

"C'mon, Martin. You know what I'm doing here. It's about Bitsy."

He nodded with a very serious face.

"I'm in love with her," he said.

"Martin, you've been in love with every woman you've ever met. You have got to let this go."

Again, the serious nod. A prodigious thinker and resolver of dilemma, he was calculating something big.

"I can't let it go. I've never felt for anyone else what I feel for her. I can't give her up, despite my friendship with you."

I was glad that I had declined the coffee.

"OK," I said. "Here's the deal: you and I have been friends for a long time. Great friends. And I truly hope that we will continue to be friends after all this is resolved. But this is not about friendship for me. This is about family, and Bitsy is my family. You know that she almost called the police? I had to talk her out of it."

This last bit of information was a body blow. It hurt him deeply.

"So here's what you need to understand, Martin," I continued. "From this moment on, if you do not back the fuck off and leave my niece alone, I'm going to come back out here and beat your ass. I hate having to tell you that, but you need to know how serious all of this is."

He blushed and broke eye contact with me.

"I'm afraid I'm going to have to ask you to leave, Conor."

I did, and despite several letters and phone calls attempting to reconnect, we did not speak for eight years.

"Conor, it's Martin calling."

"Christ, but that's something I was pretty sure I was never going to hear again. Hello."

"I'm sorry it's taken this long for me to get my head out of my ass and call you. You know, the embarrassment, the heartache. The usual residue of every romance I've ever been in."

"No apologies necessary. It's good to hear your voice."

We exchanged a few minutes' worth of pleasantries, got caught up on the high points we both had missed. Transitioning back to the closeness of our relationship was easier than I would have expected.

"What have you been doing?" I asked.

"This will clearly sound strange and out of character coming from me, but I've been working my ass off," he said earnestly.

It did sound strange and out of character. For as long as I had known him, Martin had always been the top student in his classes. Stuff just came easily to him, and the work ethic he developed as a result of this was that of a surfer born to wealthy parents. The only genuine effort I ever saw him expend was towards relationships. He would go to great lengths to plan dates, memorize details, review points of failure for future reference. It wasn't romance as much as it was process for him.

While at school getting an honors degree in literature, Martin rubbed elbows with Brendan Galway, the famous poet. Galway was a visiting scholar assigned to the Department of English and Literature. Actually, I believe Martin's interaction was all but limited to the fact that he sat in on a class taught by Galway's very young, very attractive housemate and protégé. I do not recall her name, but Martin fell deeply in love with her Dublin accent, her wild head of curly black hair and her fiery smile.

"God, he's the luckiest man on the planet," he told me after sitting in on one of her classes. "She's witty, strikingly beautiful, and she reads."

The highlight of this time was the evening we attended a cocktail party at Galway's rented home. Martin had been invited as part of the campus illuminati, and I was his guest. We drank good wine, ate designer cheese with crackers. I watched with a decent level of amusement as Martin navigated his way throughout the house in an effort to get a better look at the object of his affection. Had he been able to exchange hellos with her, I'm sure he would have fainted. Galway, our host, was witty and arrogantly aloof in appropriate dimensions.

Martin followed this poor woman around town for a couple of weeks, a clear precursor of his experience with my niece to be sure, and then he moved on. A guy who could be miserably slow on the uptake when it came to relationships, it usually took him that long to figure out that the purity of his poverty and undiluted sense of literary ambition were not what most women were looking for. I could, however, always count on him to recover. He was the most resilient bastard I had ever known.

"I don't know," he told me over beers one evening, "I just need to meet a woman who respects how much I suffer for my art."

I was tempted to ask for a description of the suffering but was pretty sure that he would take the question seriously and actually compose a list.

"You'll meet the right woman," I said. "And I've told you this before, Martin, but you have a little bit of an intensity issue. You need to back off a bit once in a while. You intimidate these women."

I was pretty sure Martin didn't intimidate anyone, least of all women. At that moment, however, he needed a bit of a lift and I knew that he would enjoy hearing this.

"You're right," he said. "It's been hard for me to maintain my equilibrium with women. I'll tell you something, my friend, those priests and nuns can really fuck you up. Great education, but lots and lots of baggage."

"It'll work out for you, Martin. Hang in there. Keep moving forward. You'll find your groove."

It did not, in fact, work out for him. He abandoned what may well have been a promising career as a literary figure and began work towards a master's degree in system science. I was not sure what, exactly, system science was, but he was the only person I knew who was capable of creating software.

A year later, broke and rather heavily in debt from school loans, he availed himself of the last safety net America had to offer middle to upper class men and women struggling to find themselves through young adulthood. Working in Central America for the Peace Corps was perfect for Martin. He made no money, but he was not expected to. He did very little work, but no one truly seemed to care. He lived in a world so slightly removed from poverty that he came to hate it. It was an epiphany; it was Paul on the road to Damascus. He returned from Central America wholly committed to getting rich and acquiring an attractive young wife. Enter Bitsy.

I remember the second time he called because of the hour, and because I was sleeping next to a Russian woman named Nadia. She and I had met a week earlier at a work gathering and had now begun enjoying each other's company for the few weeks she had remaining before going home to Moscow. Nadia's accent was exotic, and her curiosity in all things American was fetching. She was sleeping soundly beside me. I was enjoying a last moment of her nakedness lying next to me before rising to make coffee.

"It's 3:30 in the morning in California, Martin. What are you doing up?"

"I have a great idea. One that can't wait."

I climbed out of bed as quietly as I could and crept to the kitchen.

"Do you remember how we used to talk about those artist communities. What were they…in California someplace, or Colorado?"

"California," I said. "I think they were in northern California."

"Whatever. Anyway, we need to start one. You and me. It could be magical. Think about it, Conor. By the way, what are you doing these days? You know, to make a living?"

We had discussed this on our last call, but trivialities like this didn't register with him.

"I run a small TV station."

"Are you writing?"

"Not much. So, Martin, how are we supposed to finance this little project of yours?"

"Fuck that," he said. "I have that covered. This could be epic, Conor. This could be a place that truly allows young people to expand, to grow in their art."

This was vintage Martin. I smiled in the darkness.

"I'll tell you what," I said, "let's discuss this when we have a little more time. I have to get ready for work. Why don't you think about coming over for a weekend? Maybe I'll fly out to the coast. It'd be great to see you again."

The silence that ensued was predictable. Martin was digesting information about the artist community and planning his next meal simultaneously.

"I'll be there tomorrow afternoon. I need to get out of here, anyway. No need to pick me up. E-mail me your address and I'll grab a cab."

"Let me know what time your flight gets in, Martin, and I'll pick you up."

The dial tone tipped me off that the conversation was ended.

He was unchanged. The tall and lean frame had softened a bit, he had lost some hair and his face had developed deep laugh lines near the eyes. But his essence was unaltered. He scanned the airport for snipers and attractive women.

"You look good, Martin," I said as I extended my hand.

He hugged me for the first time in our lives. It lasted several seconds. I suspected that his hope was that all the lost experiences could somehow be infused into each of us through some osmotic process. Neither of us being ever inclined to this type of greeting, I must say that the moment was meaningful.

"Conor, I'm truly sorry about what happened with Bitsy. I hope you can forgive me for that."

This was rehearsed. He struggled with statements like this. He was an observer of big emotion, not a contributing participant.

"Not necessary," I said. "Let's get out of here and get something to drink."

The amount of money Martin proclaimed to have acquired was staggering. I had always associated big money with hard work or luck. Neither applied to Martin.

"Where'd it come from?"

We were driving from the airport to my apartment.

"A dot com that I built up...well, I had a few people build it for me. I'll spare you the details, but one of the big boys bought me out. They hate any hint of competition, those guys. After the nightmare with Bitsy...how is Bitsy, by the way?"

"Doing well," I said. "Married a lawyer from San Francisco. Lot's of money. I think she volunteers."

I caught him peripherally. Rejected lover deep in thought.

"Kids?"

"No. My read from a distance is that kids might get in the way. When I talked to her last...this would be several months ago...she seemed to be doing well."

We made the rest of the drive in silence. Despite our recent estrangement we had enough history to be comfortable with quiet. I suspected he would be developing the film I had just given him: beautiful young woman, handsome successful husband, nice home. He would also be reliving the break-up with Bitsy. There was no need to bother him.

As Martin showered back at my apartment, I was tempted to phone Bitsy. Had I been a bit more certain as to how all of this was going to play out, I would have. I called my office and checked on the station. Martin took forever in the shower.

Enzo's was may favorite restaurant. Only blocks away from my apartment, it had an impressive menu and was reasonably-priced. The wait staff was comprised exclusively of young and attractive women. They wore black slacks, laundered white dress shirts and completely ignored the health code requiring them to tie up their hair.

We ordered lunch salads and glasses of wine.

"You know, Conor, you've got a nice deal here. You make a decent living, you're comfortable. But I don't think you've ever really let yourself explore much. God, you wrote such great stuff when we were young."

"I think you're embellishing a bit, Martin."

"No. No. You have talent, my friend. Wouldn't it be uplifting to be able to provide support and guidance to someone developing their voice? What a legacy that would be."

I knew all along that Martin was looking for a playmate. My ability to help some young writer develop a voice was less important than my companionship.

"And it's always guys like you who propose that guys like me jump into the deep end. You don't need to worry about this little adventure failing. I do."

Martin nodded and sipped his wine.

"That makes sense. It really does. So how about we put the place entirely in your name? And I'll also start some sort of trust that will sustain it for several years. I'll make sure you're protected on this, Conor. We'll call my money guy tomorrow. He'll know how to set all of it up. I don't want you worrying about money. I need your focus on the project."

We finished lunch and walked back to my place. As Martin napped in my guest room, I had time to think. My job and the security it provided was not as grand a motivation to stay put as it might have seemed. I managed a small television station in a rather large market. The station was owned by an aging and addled guy living in Charlotte. I rarely spoke to him.

I did speak regularly to his children. They had assigned impressive corporate titles to each other and had begun sheltering the old man from the realities of the empire he had built. They drove German luxury cars and dressed in high-end suits. They knew next to nothing about the business, and it was only a matter of time until they put the old man completely out to pasture and stared selling off the silverware. My station, a going concern that lived consistently on the edge of insolvency, would be one of the first things to go.

When Martin emerged from his nap, I gave him the news that I was joining the circus. His smile was uncontained.

The next day was Saturday and we spent most of it sitting at my kitchen table making plans. We made lists for each of us. At the top of mine was a phone call Monday morning to my boss on Charlotte. He had been a very decent man to work for. So long as I made a profit, even a marginal profit, he pretty much left me alone. I knew that he would take my leaving the station personally, and this bothered me. I also knew that one of his doltish children would claim the task of finding my replacement in a truly superficial effort to appear important in the old man's eyes. God knows what kind of sycophantic kiss ass they'd install.

Martin borrowed my car late in the morning to fetch groceries. He was fired up to make dinner, and I had precious little by way of staples.

"Here," he said slapping down a piece of paper when he returned.

"What's this?" I asked.

"It's a deposit slip. I took it from your desk drawer, and just made a deposit. It's on hold for three business days, but after that, it's yours to do with what you'd like. I just don't want you to be worried about your finances, Conor. I need your focus on the project."

The largest amount of money I ever deposited at one time was usually my year-end bonus check of ten grand or so. This was ten times that amount.

"Jesus Christ, Martin. Are you sure about this?"

"Looks like we're off to the races," he said.

My Monday morning phone call with the boss seemed instantly less high a hurdle to clear.

Sugar Island is an anvil-shaped channel island in the tributary waters connecting Lakes Superior and Huron. The water rushing around each side of it is cold and clear. Ice in the winter many years ago was prodigious and lasted well into the Springtime. Much of it today is owned by the local Native American tribe.

My family has a multi-generational history on the island. My grandparents retired there. The one-bedroom cabin they occupied has gone through many upgrades and expansions as a variety of my extended family came into, and then out of, money. As it sat while Martin and I were considering sites for the community, it consisted of three bedrooms, a kitchen, a full bathroom and a glassed-in sunporch.

I can easily assemble a list of firsts in my life to have taken place there. My first books of any substance were consumed while sitting in an old Adirondack chair on the beach. I was in my first fight about a mile into the woods. I'm not certain if I won or lost, but my older cousin Wally carried a black eye around for a week or so afterwards.

When I was sixteen and very deeply in love with the daughter of my high school history teacher, I lost my virginity on Sugar Island. Nancy and I had walked to a secluded slope of hillside overlooking the water. It was a brilliantly sunny afternoon with a warming wind. I can still see her light brown hair and her ice blue eyes. As promised, I looked away as she removed her shorts and top.

We considered New Mexico, the Maritime Provinces of Canada and somewhere near Austin, Texas before settling on Sugar Island.

"My cousin and I own the place today. He'll obviously have to be consulted."

"Of course. What's the layout of the place today?"

"The main house hasn't changed much. There's a garage that we could turn into a studio of sorts. It hasn't changed much since you saw it years ago."

Martin had spent a week there with me one summer during college. He'd loved the rustic quality of the place and fell in love with every Indian girl he saw.

"Goddamn they are beautiful creatures. These are the most self-confident, strongest women on earth," he said. "They could cook me venison and mend my wounds."

"We could build a couple of dorms. One for the boys and one for the girls," he said back at my kitchen table. "We want this place to be comfortable, but not too comfortable. We want to be able to see that our artists are capable of suffering for their art."

"I know a couple builders up there...boys I went to school with. You and I will have to come up with some sort of basic floor plans, but I don't think going all in with an architect will be necessary."

"That's why this project needs you, Martin. It needs your magic."

We spread sheets of paper across the tabletop and began to sketch rooms and doorways. The thought crossed my mind, every now and then, that we should have been using crayons.

It took a couple of phone calls with my cousin and a lawyer situated in the small town nearest Sugar Island, but the deal was done relatively quickly. The place was leased to a corporation Martin and I created, and I was the major shareholder of the corporation. We had a five-year option. My cousin, who had made a small fortune developing real estate in Florida, was talking to me from a golf course he seemed to live on.

"So what is it exactly that the two of you are going to be using the old homestead for? An artist community? How exactly do you make money from something like that?"

"No money. The thing is completely self-funded by Martin. Danny, the guy's made millions of dollars."

"Martin? Martin's made some money?"

"Yeah, I know, it's wild. He got into one of those dot com things... he built it up and sold out. Anyway, we bring in talented, artsy types and give them a place to stay for a few weeks. The idea is that they can work on their craft without worrying about room and board. Hopefully, it'll help them develop as writers or painters or whatever they are."

My cousin Danny had gone from lugging cinder blocks on job sites to personally developing large and lucrative tracs of land. He was an extremely intelligent man with an innate ability to identify all the elements surrounding a concept. To him, however, an artist community was destined to remain in ether. This was a concept he elected not to understand. He could have wrapped his head around it, he simply determined that the effort necessary to accomplish this was not worth it.

"I'll take your word for it," was the best Danny could muster.

"It might work out, Danny. Hell, Martin put six figures in my bank account just to make sure I was comfortable moving forward with all of this. And you and I end up still owning the property…and it will be worth a lot more because of the renovations we're making."

"Get an accountant," he said. "That's a lot of money, and you don't want it coming back to bite your ass. Taxes and stuff."

Martin and I drove the sixteen hours from northern Virginia to the small town of Sault Ste. Marie in Michigan aided by strong and bitter cups of coffee and buoyed by a resolve we found ourselves developing mile by mile. I did most of the driving; Martin took pages of notes on a yellow legal pad that seemed sewn into the lap of his trousers.

We started with the near inconsequential stuff and worked our way up. We decided to give each member of the community a heavy hooded sweatshirt upon arrival. It gets chilly at night on Sugar Island. Within an hour we had selected green as the official community color.

Food would be left to me. I dictated a list of pastas, stews, a variety of meats, fruits and vegetables which Martin recorded.

"What if we get a vegetarian?" he asked.

It came across as if he were asking what we would do if we got a white supremacist.

"I say we ask for dietary preferences on the admission form, and we throw all the vegetarians out the window."

Martin nodded for a mile before stating his agreement. He flipped to a new page on his legal pad and wrote the word ARTIST at the top. The discussion moved to what type of creative geniuses were we willing and able to accommodate. It took us most of the state of Ohio to rule out dancers.

"I'm not saying it wouldn't be fun to have a ballet dancer around," said Martin, "but then we'd need a big room, a studio of sorts. And one of those bars on the wall. So there's that."

In the years away from him I had forgotten how much fun it could be to watch his brain work, to see how seriously he could take the tiny things, and how he shrugged away the big decisions. In the end, somewhere half-way up the Lower Peninsula of Michigan, we developed the litmus test that our artists had to be able to produce something tangible. Writers were obviously in, as were painters. Musicians, if we both liked the type of stuff they created.

He interrupted a couple more miles of silence by telling me that he was against performance art in almost every form.

"Those guys who light a fire in the middle of a stage and then piss on it to show us the significance of man's ability to control his environment...those fuckers are out."

We remember places by smell. The old house had multiple generations of my family in the air. Coffee in the morning, campfires at night.

The place wasn't nearly as finished as I had remembered, but the bones of the house were solid.

"We'll need to build an extension on this kitchen," I said.

Martin made a note.

"And I think we should have community meals, maybe around a big table with benches. And we'll need to get someone started on the dorms. I like the idea of each dorm having a bathroom, but the boys and girls could be adjacent in order to save on plumbing. I wonder how that works...will we need a new septic system?"

"Leave all that to the contractor," he said with a dramatic wave of the arm.

"You take the big room upstairs," I told him. "I would actually prefer the little room down here. It's where I used to sleep when I visited as a kid. We can turn the extra room upstairs into an office of sorts for the two of us. The sunroom will be open to anyone."

"Yes. Yes. We're going to do some real good here, Conor. Thank you for this."

Working my way upstream through the details of the project I realized that Martin and I had never spent more than a week together at one time. He had a genuine tendency to grow on a person. Not unlike a fresh puppy or a malignancy.

I flew back to Virginia a week later to finalize my move and to arrange for almost all my stuff to be placed in storage. Martin had made a hell of dent in our to-do list when I returned five days later.

One of the more appealing aspects of small-town life is the absence of red tape. Had we been building a new house, even on Sugar Island, multiple visits from the building inspector would have been necessary, permits would have been needed. But we were adding bunkhouses. We learned that the bathrooms could be tied into the existing septic system so long as we limited the number of occupants to three each. Our contractor, a salt-of-the-earth man I'd known as a kid, moved forward without so much as a phone call to any of the municipal buildings in town.

"We'll get started, and if somebody sees us working and wants us to get a permit, we'll take care of it then. Shit, this won't take ten days."

He and his crew of bearded men were finished in a week. Two bunk houses, each capable of housing three campers, twin bathrooms with showers built back-to-back, renovation of the garage into a studio, and the expansion on the kitchen area in the main house turned out better than our most grandiose expectations. A day after they were finished, a truck carrying new appliances backed down the drive. We were as ready as we were likely to get.

"Now the hard part," Martin said.

We had driven to the island's only eating establishment, The Deer Kill Bar, and were enjoying a meal of fried perch, coleslaw and beers. The Deer Kill was vintage north country. The wood paneled walls were decorated with hockey sticks, hockey jerseys and pictures of hockey players. The collection of stuffed animals was right out of taxidermy heaven. There was a handful of regulars sipping draft beer at the bar, and only one other table of diners.

The owner of the place, a man named Edward Dump, had scraped out a living for many years selling cold beer to the locals and over-priced pub food to tourists. Dump had a taste for liquor and sipped his profits away from his stool behind the bar almost every night. He also was incapable of averting his eyes from teenage girls. More than once in his career he had been compelled to make speedy apologies to a variety of fathers.

"She reminds me of my niece," he would plead.

The locals at the bar were amused by these instances. Although they had a working relationship with Dump, none of them brought their daughters into the place.

"What's the hard part?" I answered.

Now we figure out how we're going to attract the right people. I'm thinking we could start the first session in July or August. The weather will be right, and that will give us almost two months to get all of it settled."

We started the next morning. We took out advertisements in several artsy magazines. Martin created a web page in a matter of an hour. Forever a photography enthusiast, the pictures he posted were a real draw. The old homestead, in all its refinished splendor, had a lot to offer.

The Sugar Island Artist Community

Located on rustic Sugar Island in the Upper Peninsula of Michigan, our community offers serious artists a tranquil, worry-free environment. We are now accepting applications for a four- week term beginning in July.

Worry not of the travails of living, but of the travels of artistic expression.

Contact via e-mail.

"Who'd the quote come from?" I asked.
"I just made that shit up."

The Artists

The list of applicants we assembled from e-mailed inquiries surprised us, not simply by the volume, but by the apparent talent pool represented. We were limited to what we were reading and seeing as provided by the artists themselves, but we quickly developed a Yin Yang methodology in our selection process. Martin poured over each candidate's profile and submitted work with an eye toward genuine artistic ability; I looked for fakes.

"There are a lot of people out there looking for a free ride," I said.

"I don't care if they get a free ride as long as they can produce something meaningful. Besides, we can always send their asses home."

We were sitting at the huge dining table pouring over the application forms representing the final six candidates. The table was large enough to easily seat eight and was constructed of heavy and hard dark wood. We sipped beers from Canada and nibbled an acid sharp cheese like rats.

"Six might be a handful," I said, "if for no other reason, the cooking."

"Agreed. Let's go with four for the first time. And if we expand down the road, we'll hire some island girl to come in and help. Maybe an Indian woman."

"What if the best candidates are clearly all men? Or all women?" I asked.

Martin chewed on that for a few seconds. I wasn't sure of he was processing my question or still developing mental images of the island girl dancing around the kitchen.

"I think that having a mix gives us credibility," he said. "It would be weird as hell for two guys to build this place and then bring in only guy artists. We're not monks. And it would be catastrophic to bring only women in. I think we need to mix it up for appearances sake, for validation.

Emile, the first of our guests to arrive three weeks later, descended the steps from the twin engine 10-seater turboprop at the County Airport. He was directly out of central casting, easily over six feet tall, with shoulder-length black hair. He wore tight black jeans and a black cargo jacket. His backpack kept with the color scheme. He was a seriously handsome guy.

He had come to us highly praised by the Art Department at Corning Community College in upstate New York. His credentials included a showing at a small gallery in Manhattan, a batch of awards from various competitions throughout the northeast, and a self-proclaimed god-like and tireless level of energy used to infuse life into inanimate materials. A sculptor.

"Emile, welcome to the Upper Peninsula. I'm Conor and this is Martin. We run the community. We're very glad to have you here."

His handshake was firm, the skin as rough as sandpaper.

"Any other luggage?" asked Martin.

He looked immediately and directly at Martin. The focus was, to be honest, a bit intimidating. Had we not spoken to him prior to his arrival, I would have thought it possible that a deaf kid just descended the airplane steps. Such an interesting storyline, struggling through a life of teasing and chastisement only to discover as a young man that his real gift, that of creating beautiful sculptings, could carry him through life. No doubt he had used the pain and forced privacy he had endured as the genesis of the beauty he brought into the world. He wore his suffering like a mask. His face said everything.

Finally, he spoke.

"Can either of you tell me where the can is? I've had to shit for an hour."

"It's all about tension. This is what Da Vinci taught us."

Emile was explaining his creative process. He had been silent as we drove from the airport into town, but was now eagerly blessing us with his theory of art.

"Not just with sculpting things. Painters...well, good painters create it, too. But I believe it is a more important element with sculpting. Tension has to be there for the work to live."

We were eating pizza in town before heading back to the island. Afterwards, we walked through the tourist shops. Bows and arrows suitable for four-year-olds; fudge in every flavor imaginable. Every woman under the age of death ogled Emile. He genuinely didn't seem to notice or care.

I headed back to the airport the next day. We had purchased an eight-seat van for community use. Martin had had it detailed with silhouetted pine trees and *Sugar Island Artist Community* on each side. The deck hand on the ferry was interested.

"What's a Sugar Island Artist Community?"

He had lingered to chat after having collected money and tickets from those of us making the crossing. His name, he told me, was Archambault. I had known members of his family from childhood. He lived on the island...it was a rule that all employees of the ferry do so, and I was relatively certain that he made some extra cash selling pot. I'd paid attention on previous crossings and was pretty sure that I'd seen him conducting business.

"It's like a camp for artists. You know, writers, painters, those kind of people."

"Well, make sure that you tell whatever deckhand is on duty that they're kids and that it's some sort of school. You'll get a discount on the crossing."

"Thanks, but most of them will be adults. Some may even be my age, or older."

Archambault tilted his head. This information came at him from an odd angle.

"So there like special people? Is that what you call them? Like special needs people?"

"Yeah. Kind of like special needs people. We let them come here to work on their art, and hopefully they leave happier."

"That's a really nice thing for you to do," said Archambault, "and that's one hell of a van you got there."

Jeremy Vanderwheele came to us from Atlanta. He was a short, thin young man with bleached-white hair and very light blue eyes. He wore jeans, a red dress shirt and alarmingly white sneakers. The diamond stud in his left earlobe looked too big to be real. He exited the small airplane as if he had survived a flight to a South Pole research station. Jeremy was a writer of short stories, several of them published already in his young life. He expressed a desire to spend his time with us fleshing out a novel.

Monica Leanne, and she introduced herself in this manner and corrected me the first time I referred to her as simply Monica, was a painter. She had nicely styled dark brown hair, and a body that was rapidly nearing and surpassing adult womanhood. Perfect at nineteen, she appeared to carry a genetic disposition toward fullness of form. Her teeth were perfectly straight, and she had a winning smile.

She was a rising sophomore at Purity University, a Christian-based uber-conservative college in the hills of Virginia. The school was prominent in the news earlier in the year because of a campus shooting. A seriously troubled student killed three innocent bystanders in an off-campus coffee shop. Of interest, two campus police officers shot him to death on network television as he was trying to surrender. The school's president, a charter member of the National Rifle Association, as well as a major contributor to right wing radio talk shows, defended his officers with Old Testament rationalizations.

And then there was Amy. She drove up the following day with her five-year-old daughter Maura. We had given a good deal of thought about including someone with a child in tow, but Martin was persuasive in his argument that having a little girl around would add a touch of normalcy to our group.

We meet people from time to time who linger in our thinking: at night when we attempt to interpret the day's happenings; in the morning when we struggle to remember dreams that have pleased us. Amy was that person.

Not strikingly attractive, reddish brown hair and dark blue eyes, she was a Renaissance woman. She sketched, she wrote music, she was a poet. She had worked on a vineyard tying grapes and had gone through culinary school.

Her daughter Maura was a head full of crazy black hair. She was wiry and shy; she was precocious, polite and attentive. She was instantly adored by everyone except Emile. He was apparently well beyond the level of artistic entrenchment that would have allowed him to give a shit about a little girl.

Dinner that night, our first as a completed collective, was Italian sausage and peppers in red sauce served over pasta. Martin and I had gone around and around on whether to serve wine with meals.

"Conor, we have to treat these people as independent adults. If we trust them enough to bring them into the community, we should be able to trust their decision making on these kinds of things. Besides, I like a nice glass of wine with my dinner."

"No thanks," said Amy, "red wine sometimes keeps me up at night, and I need to get a good night's sleep."

Emile declined with a dismissive wave of his hand. Jeremy allowed Martin to pour him a glass, as did Monica Leanne.

"When in Rome," she said.

During dinner we established a short list of chores for each guest. We wanted to be able to provide as much time as possible for their respective creative processes but felt that a marginal contribution to the general upkeep of the place was acceptable.

Amy was an obvious candidate to help me with cooking. Monica Leanne and Jeremy volunteered to perform after-meal clean-up.

"What are you going to do, Emile?" asked Monica Leanne.

"I was rather hoping the list had been exhausted," he said.

"You can drive the trash up to the dump every other day," I said. "It's about three miles away. I'll show you where it is tomorrow. It's a nice drive and there's a good possibility you'll get to see a bear or two."

Emile shrugged.

"Good night, everyone," he said as he stood to leave.

"Emile," said Monica Leanne, "if you ever want company going to the dump, I'd love to come along."

He did not acknowledge her and walked quickly out the door toward the cabins.

Jeremy and Monica Leanne stayed up well after the rest of us had turned in. They sat at the kitchen table playing gin rummy.

"That Emile is something, isn't he?"

"I'm not sure I get a good read on him," said Jeremy. "Part of me wants to think he's just anti-social, and part of me wants to think he's an asshole."

"I don't think he's an asshole," she said, "I think he's just misunderstood. But Jesus Christ he's gorgeous."

"Girl," said Jeremy, "do not even get me started."

The next morning Martin and I visited each camper. We wanted to make certain they had what they needed and were comfortable in their respective workspaces.

The garage we would certainly need for vehicles in the event we wintered there had been turned into a studio and assigned to Emile. Martin had purchased a table sufficiently sturdy to autopsy a rhino and fitted one end of it with a large vise. Per Emile's request, we had purchased several blocks of hardwood from one of the islanders known for chainsaw carvings of bears and wolves. We thought it would be interesting to drag Emile to see the man but decided to wait to see what kind of stuff Emile produced before extending the invitation. The carvings were quite lifelike.

Emile was playing with the chisels and grinding tools when we stopped by.

"You have everything you need, Emile?" I asked.

"I won't know until I get into it. I'll make it work. What kind of wood is this, oak?"

"Yeah. It's oak that's been aged a while. We bought it from a guy who carves animals and stuff with a chainsaw. He lives on the other side of the island."

Emile did not look up from his tools. He exhaled loudly, clearly exhausted and suffering greatly at having to live his life among inferiors.

"What a condescending fuck," I said to Martin as we walked toward Jeremy.

Jeremy was typing away on his laptop when we interrupted him.

"We won't keep you but wanted to make sure you had what you needed. You seem self-contained. Need anything?"

"I might ask one of you to read along as I work on this. Most of my writing lately is done as part of classwork, so I've gotten used to the feedback."

"Martin's your guy," I said. "He was a genuine literary figure when we were in school. He got published in some very reputable magazines."

"Any advice will be appreciated," said Jeremy as he resumed working.

The barn-like structure the workmen built was divided into same-sized work areas. Both had a view of the water, and both had an abundance of natural light.

Monica Leanne was sketching with charcoal.

"May we interrupt?" asked Martin.

"Sure. Come in. I'm just playing."

"You and Emile are the lucky ones," I said. "Martin and I have zero talent in creating anything visual, so the two of you will have to struggle through the term without our sage advice."

She wore a pair of form-fitting yoga pants and a loose short-sleeved sweatshirt. She was very clearly not wearing a bra. Certain arm movements and gestures allowed for a clear vision of her underarms.

"Just wanted to make sure you had what you need," said Martin.

She placed the charcoal on the ledge of her easel and turned rather dramatically to us. She closed her eyes before speaking.

"This place is so wonderful. The two of you are such great people to be doing what you're doing, and I thank my lord and personal savior Jesus Christ for the opportunity to be here."

"Well, Monica Leanne, we're delighted you're here with us," I said.

Martin turned back towards her as we were leaving.

"Any thoughts on what you're going to work on, Monica Leanne?"

"I was thinking about a nude," she said, charcoal back in hand. "Either of you interested in posing?"

"I don't think we have the forms you're looking for," said Martin. "Maybe ask Emile."

"God, don't I wish," said the student visiting us from Purity University in the State of Virginia.

Amy's artistic expression was the most nebulous of the group. She painted, she wrote music, several of her poems had been published.

"It's almost as if she expresses her art in her every-day actions," I said to Martin. "In the way she cooks, the way she parents, in her movements."

Martin had donated his guitar to Amy's workstation. It was a high-end Martin that had recently been restrung. It rested in a guitar stand in a corner of studio.

"I rarely play the fucker anyway," he said, "maybe she'll inspire me to play more after she's gone."

In addition to a writing table, we had also installed a drafting table in Amy's area. This is where we found her sitting when we entered.

She held a drawing pencil as if holding a cigarette. She glanced to and from Maura sitting in the window nook. The likeness was remarkable. The lines of the little girl's body, the wildness of her hair, the position of her legs folded beneath her as she sat and looked out to the waterline.

"My god, that's beautiful," said Martin.

"Thanks. Just warming up a bit."

"May I have it when you're finished?" asked Martin.

"Huh?"

"I'd be humbled if you would give us that," he said. "We'd hang it in the kitchen and future guests would be able to enjoy it."

"I'll give that some thought," said Amy.

The following morning, after the breakfast dishes had been cleared and cleaned by Jeremy and Monica Leanne, we all headed into town. Emile elected to stay and work. It was already turning into a warm morning and working with the garage door opened Emile made quite an impression as he chiseled away. He wore safety goggles and no shirt.

Once parked on the ferry, we settled in for the short crossing. One of the big boats, a thousand-foot-long ore freighter was making its way up to the locks that would deliver it into Lake Superior. The prospect of gliding within a few hundred feet of it was real, and this was an experience I thought the artists should have.

"Why don't you guys get out and stand by the railing. Just get back in the car by the time we dock on the other side."

Jeremy and Monica Leanne opened the side door of the van and slipped out of the second-row seats.

"May I go, mother?"

Maura was sitting in the third row with Martin.

"I'll make a deal with you," said Amy. "If you act like a perfect little angel while we're out today, you and I will stand at the railing on the way back."

"But I'm always a perfect little angel. You told me."

"Then it should be easy," said Amy.

Archambault stopped to take our payment and to inspect the newcomers. He glanced a bit longer than was comfortable at Amy, who was sitting across from me in the front seat. Her hair was pulled up and held in place on top of her head. She wore khaki shorts, a tee shirt and sandals. He paid no attention to Martin or Maura.

"Those two standing over there are with me as well," I told him.

"How's art camp?" he asked.

"It's doing quite well," I said. "You should stop by and say hello some time."

"Maybe. See you."

Archambault zig-zagged through the parked vehicles to where Jeremy and Monica Leanne stood. Closer in age to the two of them, their conversation seemed more free-flowing than the one or two word exchange he had just had with me. They all shook hands and chatted until it was time for him to secure the boat at the other side.

In town we separated. Amy and I needed to shop for a week's worth of meals; Monica Leanne and Jeremy wanted to visit the tourist shops for souvenirs; Martin and Maura went to watch a freighter traverse through the locks and to have ice cream.

"I'll be a perfect little darling," she told us as Martin took her hand and led her down the sidewalk.

"What a sparkler of a kid you've got there," I told Amy as we pushed twin grocery carts up and down aisles.

It became evident early on that she was far more skilled than I at developing meal plans. She had worked in restaurants, and her help with the shopping was invaluable. Even with a list, I would have been sure to forget important items.

"She's easy. She witnessed what I went through with her dad, and she's looked out for me ever since. It wasn't horrible, it just wasn't good, you know? Anyway, she doesn't want to cause me any grief. How about homemade pizzas one night? They're pretty easy to do, and Maura loves to help."

"Whatever you think. We're partners in crime now."

We sped through the cookies and sweets aisle. In potato chips we added only microwave popcorn to our carts.

"You have kids, Conor?"

"Nope."

"Touchy subject? Sorry," she said.

"Not at all. I was married for a year, but my wife never quite seemed committed, if you know what I mean. Having a child with her would have been irresponsible. I think about it, though. I mean, I'm still a young man…young enough to be a father. It just hasn't happened, I guess."

"What's Martin's deal?" she asked. "Has he been married? Any kids?"

"That's a funny story I'll tell you sometime, how he wanted to marry my niece. Christ, what a clusterfuck that was. But no, he's never been married. No kids."

"He's an odd one," she said. "Nice enough, and I'm certainly grateful that the two of you allowed Maura and me to come here. He's just a little different from anyone I've been around. I can't put my finger on it."

"I've been trying to figure him out since we were seventeen years old. Let me know when you have something."

We rendezvoused at the fountain by the locks. A freighter was inching its way through.

Monica Leanne and Jeremy carried bags of trinkets. Miniature rubber tomahawks, refrigerator magnets depicting the scenic beauty that is the Upper Peninsula of Michigan, a couple of tee shirts each.

Martin and Maura were the last to join. We saw them coming down the sidewalk holding hands. Martin carried a small bag.

"Where'd you get the shirt, Maura?" asked her mother.

"We had a little accident with an ice cream cone," said Martin. "These tee shirts are cheap, and it was better than having her walk around with chocolate all over her front."

"I was a mess, mother."

True to her word, Amy and Maura stood at the railing of the ferry on the return trip. It was a windy afternoon, and Maura squealed when a large wave sprayed the two of them.

Monica Leanne joined them at the railing and chatted for a few moments before strolling toward the back of the boat. Jeremy sat in his second-row seat reading a travel magazine. Martin napped in the back of the bus.

"Oh, hey," said Jeremy, "ML and I bumped into a guy in town who was asking about the artist community. He was shopping in one of the tourist stores."

"How did he know you were associated with us?" I asked.

"He said he saw us getting out of the van."

"What did he want to know?"

"I'm not sure," said Jeremy, "but I just told him how cool you and Martin were, how nice a place it was. That kind of thing. He said he had some interest in having his kid attend someplace like this."

"Interesting."

It took some minor adjustment of the rearview mirror, but I was able to follow Monica Leanne to the back of the boat as Jeremy was telling me this. She stood alone and appeared to be admiring the scenery and the occasional light spray.

When Archambault appeared at her side I was not as much alarmed as interested. I had to wonder what they could possible have in common; she, an art student at a hard-core Christian school, quite clearly from a well-to-do family; he, a guy from Sugar Island working in a job that, if he remained very lucky, would last him the rest of his life.

The exchange of currency for a small baggie answered my question.

"Motherfucker," I whispered to myself.

"I need to talk to you about something I saw…something I may have seen on the ferry on the way back."

Amy and I were preparing dinner and had the kitchen to ourselves. Maura was sitting in the sunroom with Martin, a chess board and men set up between them.

"Yeah, I'm pretty sure I know what you're referring to. The deal made at the back of the boat?"

"Yes. Listen, I don't give a crap one way or the other. But this is your place, and I thought you should know."

"I appreciate that. I'm not sure how I'm going to handle that, if at all. If she keeps quiet about it, I'm inclined to not say anything. She's an adult."

Amy bumped me shoulder-to-shoulder causing me to side-step for balance.

"See, you might make a good father after all. Don't give up hope yet, old man."

As we entered the main stretch of our first session of The Sugar Island Artist Community, Martin and I decided to get away for a few hours to catalog successes and failures. On balance it seemed that we had a lot to pleased with. At the very least, we seemed to have done a good job in the selection process. To a person, the artists were putting forward the work.

We popped in on Emile as we headed to my car. His garage studio now housed four small sculptings: three busts and a cube of sorts. Although they were all carved out of oak, each held a uniqueness that impressed us.

"What are you going to do with them?" asked Martin.

"I've already spoken to the college. They'll pay to have them shipped back. I'm doing a show in the Fall.

"Feel free to leave one here if you'd like. It would certainly be a nice contribution to our place here," said Martin.

Emile smirked and went back to his chisels.

"I wonder if all sculptors are assholes, or if it's just him?" I asked as we left the studio.

Jeremy had shared his work all along, mostly with Martin. It was a coming-of-age story with a clearly biographical leaning. I was impressed with the way he outlined the entire story before beginning to write it. Martin raved about his ability to balance phrases and wording. Jeremy was a very sound writer and pounded out a thousand words a day like clockwork.

Monica Leanne's work was truly artistic. There were several charcoal landscapes of the waterline, of the big boats a mile out, of the ferry. There was one of Emile, certainly done without his knowledge or permission. In it, his artist hair hung freely over his face as he bent over a carving. Perhaps wasted on me, it was rather obviously intended to be erotic.

The three paintings were brilliant with color and texture. Her depiction of the northern lights was as ethereal and unreal as they actually are.

"Monica Leanne, these are truly wonderful," I said. "You are a very talented woman."

"Thank you. I do it for Christ."

"I'd like to photograph these for the website," said Martin. "Would you be amenable to that, Monica Leanne?"

"Of course," she said. "By the way, unless either of you would rather I didn't, I was going to hang out for a while tonight with the guy from the ferry. He's nice, and he invited me to play pool and have a couple beers at the Deer Kill."

"You're a big girl," said Martin.

Amy's artistic expression was less formulaic than that of her fellow artists. She had done several sketches, many of them of her daughter. She had written and illustrated a children's book about an elf-child living in a tree that was doomed to be chopped down. She played Martin's guitar in the afternoons when Maura napped. She also kept a detailed journal of daily life at the compound.

"Once I get home, I'll clean it up a bit and send you a copy. It might help you with future sessions."

"You're like a scribe who cooks," I told her.

I had enjoyed getting to know Amy, watching the way she raised her daughter, spending time grocery shopping and cooking with her. She was different from anyone I had known. She possessed a quiet energy and seemed perfectly contented with who she was. She was careful with confidences and was a very good listener.

Martin and I drove to the ferry and crossed into town. I wanted to drive to the next of the Channel Islands about an hour away. The place was remote, but I wanted to pay my respects to relatives buried there.

We stopped at a tiny store across the road from the four-car ferry dock to buy beers and sandwiches. We sat at a picnic table next to the dock and enjoyed the view. A big boat passed slowly by only yards from the shoreline.

"They dredge a channel out there. If they didn't do that these freighters would have to go all the way around the island," I explained.

"Why don't we go over?" asked Martin.

"It's an all-day adventure," I said. "This ferry only runs once in the morning and then once each evening. I just wanted to see it."

We made lists of good and bad without Martin's legal pad. We gave ourselves a good grade for the accommodations and the food. I floated the idea of having Amy back in the event we decided to have another session. Martin jumped on that.

"Maybe a kiln," he said, "for the next session."

"So we've decided to have one?" I asked.

Martin was wearing his serious face.

"Of course," he said. "This is our calling now, Conor."

"We'll have to close the place down over the winter. Maybe next Spring? April?"

I'd been giving some thought to what I would do over the winter. The artists were, among other things, an interesting distraction from the fact that Martin and I had never been around each other for so long.

"This isn't bullshit," I said to him, "but I feel really good about what we've accomplished here. I mean, these kids have excelled. We gave them that."

We sat through a few moments of silence and sipped at our beers.

"What are you going to do over the winter?" I asked.

"I don't know. Maybe go back to the coast. I've always got business I can busy myself with for a while. How about you?"

"My cousin Danny is always bugging me to visit him in Florida. Maybe I'll learn to golf."

It was almost dark when we pulled back into the compound. Amy sat at the large table reading. Maura slept curled up in an easy chair in the sunroom. She was covered with a multi-colored afghan.

"Where is everybody?" I asked.

"The boys are in their cabin. Monica Leanne is out. Have you eaten?"

"We grabbed burgers on the way back. Everything alright here?"

"Yeah. I made pizzas tonight. You guys don't know what you missed."

Martin checked on Maura and proclaimed that he was off to bed. I joined Amy at the table.

"We were talking about having another session in the Spring," I said. "It looks like we're going to shoot for April."

The room was dark except for the reading lamp. Amy placed her book on the table and nodded as she looked up.

"That's good. I think you guys have done some really good stuff here. Emile's a dick, but other than that we have all gotten along pretty well. And I think everyone has been able to produce. That's all on you guys. We owe that to you two."

We heard Martin's bedsprings above us.

"Let me ask you something? I said. "Don't misinterpret this, but would you have any interest in coming back up for the next session? I mean, you've been a tremendous help with the cooking and all of that. And my partner seems to have fallen in love with your daughter."

She smiled.

"People always ask not to be misinterpreted only when there are multiple possible interpretations. Why don't you tell me which one you want me to go with? And yes, I would be interested in coming back."

"Let's go with we make a good pair in the kitchen. If all else fails, we could start a diner in town and sell deer burgers."

"Imagine my relief," she said. "I thought for a minute there that you were going to tell me you were growing fond of me."

"Not a chance," I said.

We were interrupted by a pickup truck pulling in at the top of the drive. A few seconds after hearing a door open and close Monica Leanne joined us.

"Did you wait up for me? That was so thoughtful of you."

"How was your evening?" I asked.

"It was fun. We hung out at the Deer Kill and played pool, drank a few beers. They didn't even ask for ID. I met some of the islanders. Lots of beards and hooded sweatshirts."

"Join us," said Amy. "We're just chatting."

Monica Leanne took a seat at the table. Her mouth was red, almost bruised. Her lips looked chapped. I wondered if Amy noticed.

"What's Archambault like?" I asked. "I knew his cousin growing up."

"Lester? He's a nice guy. He told me if I come back in the Winter, he'll take me ice fishing."

She was tipsy from drinking and spoke with a slightly thick tongue.

"Chances of that are nil," she said, "but it was a nice offer. Well, I'm off to bed. Oh, wait, I saw that guy from town tonight. The guy that Jeremy and I met who was asking about the Artist Community. He was at the bar and came over to say hello."

"What's he look like?" I asked.

"About your size, a little on the heavy side. Gray hair."

"He tell you his name?"

"Barton. Barnett. Something like that."

She steadied herself by running her hand along the countertop on the way to the door. I stood at the window and watched her until her cabin light was turned on and then off.

"You think Monica Leanne and the ferry guy...?" asked Amy.

"Nights on Sugar Island make people act crazy sometimes," I said. "Let's turn in. You want me to carry Sleeping Beauty to your cabin for you?"

"I got her, but thanks," she said.

The Last Supper

"So, Emile, you want to exchange contact information with everyone? Martin asked smiling.

"Yeah, Emile," I added, "we feel like we haven't been able to get to know you at all. You've been a hermit here."

"I've had work to do," he said. "I came to work, not make new friends. But I must say you all have been very nice."

"I've enjoyed getting to know all of you, too," said Monica Leanne. "Martin and Conor, thank you both so much for having us. I'll pray for you."

We enjoyed sautéed whitefish and oven roasted baby potatoes as we solidified plans for departure. Emile, Monica Leanne and Jeremy were on the same flight out in the morning. Amy had agreed to stay on for a day or two to help shipping works of art to their respective owners before driving out. I was going to catch a flight in a day or two to Florida. My plan was to spend a couple weeks with my cousin before returning to help Martin close the place down for the Winter.

"And, Amy, thank you so much for helping out with all of these wonderful meals," said Monica Leanne. "You should open a restaurant."

"It's been discussed," said Amy without looking at me.

"Can I ask you a question, though? I mean a somewhat serious question?" asked Monica Leanne.

"Sure," said Amy.

"Have you ever given any thought to raising your daughter in the lord's light? I mean, having her baptized, attending a church service?"

"Yes, I have," said Amy, "but I've decided not to. If that works for you, I'm happy for you. But my experience tells me that it's not what I want for my daughter right now."

"What experience would that be?" asked Monica Leanne.

"You know, Monica Leanne, I would really prefer not to have this conversation with you right now. I respect your beliefs...I really do...I'll just ask that you respect mine and change the subject."

"That's fine," said Monica Leanne. "I was just curious. And maybe if some of the life decisions you've made were different, then these experiences you're mentioning would be different, too."

Amy took a deep breath. She chewed at the side of her mouth.

"You mean like drinking, smoking pot and pre-marital sex, Monica Leanne? Tell me something. How are those life decisions working out for you? Keeping you in the lord's light, are they?"

Monica Leanne carefully dabbed a corner of her mouth with her napkin. She rose from the table and walked to the door.

"Good night, everyone," she said. "Amy, I'm terribly sorry if I offended you."

She walked crying to her cabin. Those of us still at the table sat in silence as if we'd just seen a knife fight.

The knock on Monica Leanne's door twenty minutes later startled her. Emile stood in the darkened doorway.

"You alright?" he asked.

"I made a fool of myself," she said. "I'm passionate about my love of Jesus Christ. I can't keep it inside all of the time. And I keep forgetting that there are people who will judge me for that…who hold that up to ridicule."

He said nothing, but gently took her shoulders in his large sculptor's hands. He moved her towards him and kissed her.

"Oh my gosh," she said.

Later, when they were lying naked in her bed, she asked him if he had ever wanted to try anal.

Amy and Monica Leanne hugged the next morning. Luggage was loaded into the back of the van, and I drove the three artists to the airport. I was disappointed that Archambault was not on duty. The departure scene that could have provided would have been fun to watch.

Amy, Maura and Martin remained on the island packing artwork for shipment. It was eerily silent in the van on the way back.

"I'm going to go ahead and catch a flight to Florida tomorrow or the next day," I said when I got back to the island.

"Where in Florida?" asked Amy.

"On the Gulf side. Near Tampa. He has a place on the water."

"There are sharks in the water," said Maura.

"They would eat you," said Martin, "because you're so sweet."

"They wouldn't eat you, Maura," said her mother. "We wouldn't let them, would we?"

Amy and Maura agreed to stay on for a few days to help finalize the packing and shipping.

"We'll stay as long as we're needed. We're flexible, aren't we, Maura?"

Two days later Amy drove me to the airport. Martin and Maura were going to spend the morning on a jigsaw puzzle, and then watch a movie on television. The day was dreary as a cold wind blew in off the water.

"Before you get out of town and leave all the heavy lifting to me, I want you to know how much I've enjoyed coming here and getting to know you," she said as we sat parked on the ferry.

Although we were not moving, she held the van's steering wheel at ten and two. Her eyes were locked straight forward.

"I was hoping that you'd tell me something along those lines. Maybe I'll come and see you when I get back. Where are you going to be?"

"I have a job in Columbus, Ohio, teaching art at a day care. Not high on my list of career goals, but it will give Maura a solid place for a while. I don't need to make a lot of money."

"But you'll keep us in mind for the next session, right?"

"For sure," she said.

My flight was delayed, then cancelled, then back on again, then cancelled. I called Martin and told him that Amy and I were going to hang out in town for the four hours until the next flight out. There were plenty of flights from Detroit to Tampa, so making a connection was not going to be an issue.

Moments after hanging up, they announced that my flight was back on, and that we would be boarding in a few minutes. Amy and I looked at each other without smiles.

"Oh well," I said, "I have your number. I'll call you so long as you promise to answer."

"I would like that," she said. "Here, I have something for you."

She tied a leather bracelet around my right wrist. Never much for jewelry, I liked the way it looked.

"There, now you're cool."

"I feel cool. Thank you."

We did the cheek-to-cheek friendship kiss. She smelled like cold water.

"Listen." I said, "I'm going to give you a movie kiss now. It'll be mouth to mouth, but with lips closed. Think Rock Hudson and Doris Day."

It was soft and moist and warm. I walked across the tarmac a man filled with possibilities.

Amy picked up milk at the grocery store and headed for the ferry. She was glad to have a bit of time alone to process. She had not come to the community for anything but an interesting experience for herself and her daughter. That she had certainly found. A relationship, at least the beginnings of one, had caught her off-guard.

Her plan was to finish packing up the artwork that afternoon and leave in the morning. It was an eight hour drive to Columbus, where she and Maura would check into an extended stay hotel while looking for an apartment.

The kitchen and sunroom were empty when she entered. Her car and mine were parked in the drive. Her first thought was that Martin and Maura might have gone for a walk.

She sat at the table and reviewed the film of saying goodbye at the airport once more. The muffled sound of Martin's voice coming from upstairs interrupted the moment.

"What are you doing?" she screamed. "God damn you, what are you doing?"

The scene she walked in on in the upstairs bathroom was this: Maura sat in a tubful of water and suds. Martin sat on the floor outside the tub and was running a wet washcloth over her tiny flat chest and down into the submerged parts of her little body. He was naked and had an erection.

"This isn't what you think it is," he said as he grabbed a towel. "She spilled a drink. This isn't what it looks like, Amy."

Amy didn't speak. She picked her daughter up out of the tub and held her wet body tightly.

"I'm so sorry," she whispered into the little girl's ear.

Martin quickly pulled on a pair of pants and followed them downstairs. His dark hair was wet and stuck to the sides of his head. He wore the towel like a shawl around his shoulders.

"Please, Amy. Let me talk to you. You have to understand."

He followed her to her cabin. She turned to him as she opened the door. She had not put Maura down.

"Leave us alone. Don't come in here. We're leaving."

He stood outside the cabin and waited. He could hear movement inside as Amy quickly crammed their belongings into suitcases and backpacks. Maura was crying.

It took her longer than normal to load their belongings into the car. She would not put Maura down, and carried her on every trip from the cabin to the car and back. Martin stood in the driveway shaking his head.

"Amy, please."

She loaded Maura into the back seat and strapped her in. She did not look back for an instant as she headed for the ferry.

After parking on the ferry and turning off the engine, she brought Maura into the front seat. They both cried.

"What is happening to us?" asked Maura.

"We have to leave, honey. That's all. Nothing's happening to us. Momma's never going to leave you again."

"Please be OK, mother. Please don't cry."

When Archambault stopped to collect money for the crossing, Amy asked him for directions to the police station.

The Verdict

The message was waiting for me when I clicked over from airplane mode on my phone. It wasn't Amy. It was the police.

Martin was in custody with a bail hearing scheduled for the next morning. Amy and Maura were checked into a motel in town.

"I'm sorry, but I can't tell you where they're staying. That's their business, and I'm not sure they should be bothered right now."

She did not answer her cell any of the twenty or so times I called it. My voice messages, frantic as I have ever sounded, were not returned.

I was able to catch the turnaround flight out of Detroit and took a cab to the police station.

The cop at the front desk was beefy. It had been a while since he was required to run a mile in under ten minutes. When I told him who I was there to see, he very clearly stiffened.

"You can see him tomorrow. Nine to eleven."

I felt implicated through association.

I dialed Amy again and didn't get an answer.

I walked the three miles to the ferry dock carrying my bag, and then the five miles to the compound on the other side. The doors to Amy's cabin and to the main house were closed, but not locked. Amy had clearly left in a hurry. Sketch pads, toys and trinkets Maura had acquired from gift shops, several items of clothing all had been left behind. The house was neat. A carton of milk was on the table; I put it in the refrigerator. The tub upstairs was filled with cold water; I emptied it.

My phone rang in the middle of the night.

"Thank God," I said. "Where are you? Are you alright?"

"I'm sorry to wake you…"

"Don't be," I said. "Where are you? I need to see you?"

"It's three in the morning," she said. "We're at the Lakeside Motor Lodge. Just come over later this morning. M's sleeping."

I lay in total darkness as I talked to her. My mind raced at light speed.

"Can you tell me what happened?" I asked.

"Tomorrow. Come over about seven-thirty. I'm exhausted. And very sad."

The policeman at the desk had told me that Martin had been charged with sexual assault of a minor. I got up to make coffee. Sleep was not an option.

Amy looked beaten when she answered the door four hours later at the motel. Her eyes were red, and her lids were swollen.

"Hi, Conor," said Maura. She wore a tee shirt and shorts and was propped on both elbows watching television from one of the beds. The second bed had not been slept in.

"Good morning, Maura. Did you sleep well?"

She nodded and returned her focus to the television.

Amy and I stood outside the room, the door slightly open. She told me what had happened. It took a while, as she stopped to cry and blow her nose repeatedly. She was less than responsive when I tried to hug her.

"I'm sorry," she said, "I'm in defense mode."

"You're the last one who needs to be sorry. What can I do?"

"Buy us breakfast. Maura's hungry. We didn't really eat dinner last night. Thank God she doesn't really know what's going on."

"I don't know what I can say."

"She was obviously curious about going to the police station. What a nightmare…I never want to do that one again. I'm taking her to some social services place later this morning. Apparently, it's less traumatic for the child if the questioning…the interview is done in a normal setting. Fuck, what a nightmare."

I took her hand. Unsoft and moistened from blowing her nose.

"You need to know I will do anything in my power to make this right. I take full responsibility, and I will not leave you to have to figure any of this out on your own."

"I know," she said. "Buy Maura some pancakes and we'll go from there."

I drove Amy and Maura to a touristy restaurant on the water so that we could watch any big boats making their way through the locks. We ate pancakes and bacon. Maura wanted to know why she and her mother had slept in a motel.

"I thought you would like it, M. We're going to be leaving for Columbus very soon, and I thought we needed a practice night or two in a motel. Was it fun?"

"It was fun. Are we going back across the ferry today?"

"I'm not sure. We'll have to wait and see how today goes. Eat your breakfast, sweetheart. We have a meeting with someone in a half hour."

"I feel raw inside," she told me as we waited at the County Social Services office. Maura and Eartha Minty, the woman assigned the unenviable task of determining if a child had been molested, sat cross-legged on the floor. Amy and I watched the proceedings through the glass partition. Eartha held a cloth doll and was asking questions Amy and I could not hear. When she passed the doll to Maura, her little hand appeared to wash the chest, the back and the genital area of the doll.

I placed my hand on Amy's shoulder, but she shrugged it away. She was stiff as concrete.

"I want to kill him," she said.

"I don't think we're going to get the chance," I said.

Amy decided to stay in town another night.

"I think we need a little more practice staying in a motel," she told her daughter.

"I just can't face it there right now," she whispered to me.

I took them shopping for overnight items Amy had left behind on the island: toothbrushes, pajamas, a board game for Maura.

"This is probably going to hit the newspaper this evening," I told Amy. "A place this small...this will be big news."

"Your artist community will be fucked," she said.

"Good."

I drove back to the compound, stopping to pick up a couple bottles of wine. Inside the main house I climbed the stairs to Martin's room. Normally a very neat person, it was obvious that had left in a hurry.

Drawers remained open; clothes were on the floor. I was more in a state of disbelief than anger. I wondered how it had gone when the police showed up to take Martin away. He would have been silent.

I gave some though to burning the place down, but opted for a burger and beer at the Deer Kill. The place was nearly empty. I ordered at the bar and carried my beer to a window table to wait for my dinner. I was approached by a man I didn't recognize.

"Conor? May I join you for a few minutes?"

He was my age, more salt than pepper hair, the guy Monica Leanne and Jeremy had described.

I motioned for him to sit.

"Richard Bennett," he said. "I understand you've had some unfortunate developments. I understand that your business partner is in custody."

"You understand a lot," I said. "What can I do for you?"

"I'd like to tell you a little story, and then I'm going to go away. Nothing against your town here, but I have things to do back in California."

"I'm all ears."

"Your friend Martin is a child molester. He was arrested for this same type of thing four months ago in California. The DA's office didn't handle the case very well, and your friend hired himself a high-priced lawyer. Anyway, he walked. He left the state rather abruptly as soon as he could. It took me a while, but I located him here...with you."

"So who are you?" I asked.

"The child's grandfather...in California...let's just say he's a client of mine. I was hired to locate your friend and report back."

"So you're like a hitman or something? And stop calling him my friend. Pop his ass for all I care."

"That's not in the cards at this point. Even though what I've just told you won't be admissible in a court of law, I'm going to make certain it's known to the authorities. Small town justice doesn't always follow the same rules in cases like these. If he walks on this, I'll be there to greet him."

"Why are you telling me this?" I asked.

"I've been directed to. At the end of the day, however this shakes out, this pig does not need any help from you."

"Trust me," I said, "he's not going to get any."

The case against Martin was an exercise in rapid-fire law enforcement. The County Judge, a large woman name Marjory Red Cloud, kept a tight schedule. Well over six feet tall, Judge Red Cloud had made a name for herself as a tribal prosecutor. She had seen her share of drunken and abusive fathers and husbands and harbored no sympathy for Martin or his kind. Jury selection was speedy, and cases presented by both sides were timed. Martin, although clearly capable of hiring a top defense lawyer, stuck with the public defender assigned to him. Timothy Grundt, Esquire, had been granted the unenviable opportunity to defend someone who allegedly felt up little girls.

On cue, the DA raised the question of Martin's acquittal in California. Both attorneys sat opposite Judge Red Cloud's desk in her chambers.

"Your Honor," said Grundt, "counsel is aware that this episode in California is not admissible."

The DA was a young and handsome man of Finnish ancestry. He had attended the University of Michigan School of Law and had returned home to practice. He was tall, very fit, with dark hair and darker eyes. He wore a blue tailored suit and light brown shoes. His tie was knotted perfectly.

"Your Honor," he said, "the defendant may well have been acquitted in a similar case in California on technical issues. I've read the transcript of that case, and it appears certain that the trial itself was mishandled. Additionally, the victim's parents refused to cooperate. Understandably, their child had been through something horrific. I'm fully aware, as counsel has suggested, that the defendant's previous case should not be admitted in normal circumstances. I believe, however, that the severity of this allegation warrants inclusion of the previous case and its findings."

"No," said Red Cloud. "Let's go. We're done here. The clock is ticking, boys."

Small towns being what they are, every juror assigned to the trial had been fully apprised of the case in California. It was not clear to anyone how this information had been made available. The jurors did not speak of it, but they all knew.

One day later, both legal sides having completed their questioning in line with Judge Red Cloud's timetable, the jury heard closing arguments, also timed. It took slightly less than two hours for conviction.

Amy and I had sat together throughout the trial. When it was finished, we collected Maura from Eartha Minty's office and headed back to the island. I offered to pay for a motel, but Amy indicated that it was not necessary.

"We have to get on with things," she said. "We're expected in Columbus."

"This place is dead," I said. "I don't know if I'll ever be able to come back here."

Maura was watching television in the sunroom as her mother and I drank hot tea at the kitchen table.

"We'll leave in the morning," said Amy. "I know what you mean. I want to put this behind us soon as possible. What will you do, Conor?"

"I talked to my cousin. You know what? He wasn't surprised by all this shit with Martin. Anyway, I'm going to go spend some time at his place. Look for a job. Figure it out."

They left the next morning. Maura vibrated from the excitement of more motel rooms and a school with other children. Amy cried.

"I have no words for any of this," she said.

"I know. It went from being so comfortable…"

"Let's stay in touch please," she said. "Give us a little time to settle. Call me from Florida."

She kissed the corner of my mouth as we hugged goodbye.

I stood at the end of the drive and watched her car move steadily away down the long, straight road to the ferry dock. I thought I noticed break lights, but was convinced that she must have been avoiding a squirrel when she didn't turn around.

MADELEINE'S GHOSTS

"IT'S LIKE THAT OYL GIRL and her baby," my father was saying as I entered his hospital room. "Probably a lot of people in that town had ideas about who the father was. But in those days, people had the decency to keep those thoughts to themselves."

He was sharing this insight with Beth, the tall and rock-star thin nursing aid who had come to remove his lunch tray. She wore elaborate tattoos on each arm and had multiple piercings in both ears. She smiled at my father as a reflex; she had no idea what he was talking about.

"It's from an old television show," I said. "Popeye the Sailor. He's talking about Olive Oyl, Popeye's girlfriend. She had a baby boy she lugged around. I don't think it was ever explained who the father was."

"I think I was dreaming," said my father.

This was standard fare the last week or so of his life. His lungs lost their ability to process enough air, and his heart slowly lost the strength to push oxygen to his brain. Dreams crept over and back across the line of consciousness, and the resulting subject matter of his statements reflected this. His reality had very few boundaries.

"Sounds like a good show," said Beth.

Dad smiled, clearly enjoying his own dreamspeak.

"Check it out, Beth," he said. "You don't know what you're missing, love."

I was extremely lucky to have these last days with my father. Had my brother and I been girls, dad might well have dedicated more time to us growing up. Had our interests run more toward ballet recitals instead of baseball games, he may have been more inclined to show support or genuine interest.

But he was old school when it came to raising boys. His logic must have been that my brother and I would have to be self-sufficient eventually, and that there was no reason to delay that timeline. He was as good a father as he probably knew how to be, but he was distracted easily; substantive conversations were rare.

So these last days were like gifts. I saw a side of my father that I didn't know existed. Night after night, tiny Christmas tree lights from the monitoring devices blinking red and green, I sat and watched him dream. When he woke, he would interpret what he had just lived in his mind's eye, often with laughter or serious introspection. Only rarely did he acknowledge that he was stumped by the subject matter.

"I have no fucking clue what any of that one meant," he'd say.

But in these last days and nights I learned who my father had been. It was not that he made the decision to allow me access; quite simply, his life bled over the boundaries he had established and maintained for all those years. I learned of his life as a young man, as a husband to my mother (rest in peace), of his infirmaries and infidelities. And I watched him slowly coming to grips with the fact that he would soon be dead. He oozed dignity with each day's decline.

They brought the old lady in on a Friday night. I was reading, and dad was slipping in and out of a dream that seemed to change characters from moment to moment. Dinner trays had been served and collected, and the hospital was easing into the nighttime rhythm in which most visitors find comfort. In the slower pace of the darkened hallways and rooms, visitors allowed their false fronts to fall away. Those sitting vigil could allow feelings they had hidden from the glare of the light to find freedom through the pores of their faces. There could be the release of tedium, irritation, love, fear and loss without the consequences of discovery.

The two hospital workers lifted her into her bed with as little effort as they would expend in a week. She could not have weighed 75 pounds and appeared as close to death as anyone I had ever seen. Her white hair was as sparse as an infant's, and her cheek bones threatened to puncture through her parchment skin at any moment. Her eyes were closed, and her mouth remained slightly opened. Her narrow and colorless lips were as dry as the desert.

I liked it that the hospital workers spoke to the old lady through the whole process. Although she was clearly not conscious, it was comforting to think that some of the kind and gentle words were finding their way to wherever she was.

Dad had drifted off, and I headed to the cafeteria for my own dinner. I called my brother from the hallway.

"Billy, you probably want to think about getting down here sooner rather than later," I said. "Nobody's really giving me a timeframe here, but he seems to be having more difficulty with his breathing. I don't know, it's like he's making a decision to go, if that makes sense."

"How is he mentally?" Bill asked. "Is he lucid?"

"That's the funny part…he's a bit in and out of it. But I gotta tell you, this is the most enjoyable time I've ever spent with him. It's like he has no interest in being a dad right now. He's just enjoying being able to unload. He's telling me stuff he never would have before."

"What's he talking about? Confessional stuff?"

"Being a kid in the war, being a father at such a young age. You know, he really wasn't ready for that and I think he's trying to tell me that he knows he made mistakes."

"Like an apology?"

"No. For sure it's not an apology. Maybe the opposite. Maybe he's just sharing the fact that he was who he was, and that if I have a problem with that…well, that's on me. Or us."

"Is he comfortable?"

"For the most part. Like I said, he gets out of breath easily, but nothing other than that. His appetite's good. Hits on the nurses. You know."

Billy's stern and serious face was staring at me through the cell phone airways at this last comment.

"Has he talked about Madeleine?"

"A bunch. Especially about the beginning and the end. How pretty she was. And this is cool: he's convinced that her ghost has been visiting him regularly. Like on a daily basis."

"She's probably looking for him to beat his ass for all the screwing around he did."

I thought about that for a moment before responding. Dad had been a man of his time. Fidelity had been no more a practiced art then than it is today, but periodic indiscretions were perhaps more easily waved off in those times. I was not of the mind to brush away the impact of an unfaithful spouse…I knew something about that from my own failed marriage…I just think that the last couple of days in the hospital with him had softened me a bit on this subject. It clearly remained an exposed nerve with my brother.

I also thought about the fact that dad was convinced he was being visited from the afterworld. After her death, we had all experienced her essence, the sense of her being in a room with us. In the aftermath of my divorce from Maria, I was pretty certain it was Madeleine pulling the strings necessary for me to suspend my inclination to drink myself to death.

"Well," I said, "it'll be back to normal for the two of them in the afterworld, won't it?"

"See you in a couple days," said my older brother.

My ritual had become to eat a light dinner in the cafeteria, bring a cup of coffee back to dad's room, and spend an hour or so with him before heading out to my apartment. It was peaceful sitting in his darkened room. Only the chirping from the monitoring devices and an occasional visit from the nurse for vitals broke the spell.

I wasn't sure if the person sitting in the easy chair beside the old woman's bed was a man or woman, boy or girl. It was dark, and about all I could really take in was the extremely short hair.

"Hello," she said in a whisper.

I nodded and sat down with my coffee. Dad was sleeping soundly, but still had his light snoring periodically interrupted by seemingly nonsensical statements.

"Wait a second…"

"That's OK…"

As often as not, these statements would be followed by low key laughter. As if he'd caught himself in another dream and found the entire process amusing.

"My father is a bit in and out of la-la land," I said. "He's doing a lot of dreaming and the dreams are spilling over the edges. Let's hope he doesn't say anything too outrageous."

She smiled in the darkness.

"You're lucky he can talk to you at all," she said. "My grandmother… well, she's not really my grandmother, won't ever be able to speak again. At least that's what I've been told."

"I'm very sorry for you," I said, "nothing prepares us to be able to deal with this kind of stuff, does it?"

"Can you tell me where the bathroom is?"

"Yup. Left in the hall, through the big doors, and then on your right."

As she entered the light at the edge of the room, I picked up on the hair before anything else. Short and very dark red. Her complexion was chalky; she easily could have been an understudy for an actress in the role of Queen Elizabeth. The wardrobe was right out of Salvation Army.

She sat with her legs curled up beneath her when she returned. It was in this same position that I found her the next morning.

One of the hospital staff had given her a green blanket, and she slept very delicately under it. The light had not yet come up in the room, and I was careful not to make a sound as I took my seat. Dad slept quietly, pursing his lips a bit with each exhale.

Dad and Queen Elizabeth were wakened by the delivery of breakfast. There was only one tray; apparently, the woman sharing Dad's room was getting whatever nourishment she might possibly need through the IV tubes. She appeared to have lost weight overnight. Although the Queen had told me the night before that there was not hope of recovery for the woman, it sank in fully as I looked at her in the morning light. The stroke, or whatever it was that put her in this place of no return, had done its worst. And the worst had been bad enough. I looked at the Queen as she stretched her legs out from under her, and I wanted to hug her.

"Good morning," I said.

She nodded as she stood and stretched her spine for the first time in several hours. In the light of the morning I catalogued her clothing: jeans that were badly faded with holes at each knee, a sweatshirt at least two people too large, well-worn but expensive running shoes.

"Hi again," she said.

I spoke to Dad while the Queen was away using the restroom. He had not had a good night. His eyes were milky blue with light touches of red infused. Gravity had a firmer hold on his face today than it did yesterday. He was stoic when I asked how he felt, but I could sense that he had slipped not insignificantly overnight.

He perked up when the Queen returned.

"Hello, love. I'm George. In case you haven't met, this is my favorite youngest son Matthew."

The Queen smiled.

"I'm Mary, and this is Elaine," she said motioning to the other bed in the room.

"She alright, sweetie?" asked Dad.

"She's had a stroke. I'm moving her...they're moving her to a hospice today or tomorrow. But thanks for asking."

"She's a very lucky woman to have someone like you looking out for her in her final hours. When the Father comes by later, we'll ask him to say a prayer for her."

Mary smiled slightly and returned to her chair. Dad watched the news on television with his milky eyes. He didn't react to much of what came to him over the airwaves. He dozed off and on.

"Madeleine," he said softly.

He looked directly at me. His level of alertness had risen.

"Your mother was just here. She's been visiting me a bit lately. She tells me things sometimes, but not today. I think she was just letting me know that the time was near."

"Time for what, Dad?"

"Time to put me on the bus and say a prayer for me."

"You were dreaming," I told him.

Mary looked at Dad the entire time. Her white face was calm, and her light blue eyes were focused. When he had drifted back to sleep, she stood and gazed out the window.

"I'm going downstairs for a cup of coffee, "I said. "Want some?"

"I actually would love a cup of coffee, but I didn't bring any money," she said. "Actually, I don't really have any money, but I could pay you back."

She was not the least bit embarrassed.

"So you've been sitting here for 16 hours with nothing to eat or drink?"

"I ate the fruit cup from your Dad's snack after you left last night."

She smiled as she told me this. Again, no embarrassment or awkwardness.

"C'mon. I'll buy you a cup of coffee and a muffin. We can't have you stealing from the patients."

The cafeteria staff was enjoying the downtime between the morning breakfast crowd and lunchtime. All but a couple tables were empty.

I grabbed a tray and placed two sets of silverware on it. Mary stepped in line behind me.

"Would you like some real breakfast, Mary. The muffins look good, but I'd like to buy you a real meal if you'd like."

"Just a muffin, thank you. Blueberry please."

We sat and sipped our coffee and ate our muffins. Mary sat cross-legged in the booth opposite me. We listened to the voices coming through the loudspeakers; we did not know the codes, but like all hospital visitors, we knew the floor holding our loved ones.

Mary's muffin was gone in seconds. She pressed her finger to the plate to grab up the crumbs.

"Are you sure you don't want something more to eat, Mary? You must be famished."

"I'm fine, thank you. But I'll eat the rest of your muffin if you don't want it."

Watching her eat the bottom half of my muffin was as enjoyable a moment as I'd had in years.

"We must have won the war with the Indians."

This is what Dad was telling us as we returned from the cafeteria.

"What war?" I asked. "What're you talking about?"

"The nurse who was just in here was a white girl. What happened to all the Indians? I think they used to own this place. There must have been some sort of war and the white people won."

"You're dreaming, Dad," I said as I looked directly at Mary.

He took a few seconds for that to fully finds its way in. He shook his head.

"That was an odd one."

I explained to Mary that Dad had grown up in a part of the country with a very large Native American population. Later in his life, the

Indians had actually bought up many of the town's infrastructure, hospital included.

"Please tell this girl that I'm not a racist, will you?"

Mary smiled with closed thin lips.

"I wonder if Elaine is dreaming," she said. "That would make me feel good, to think that she might be dreaming."

"What would she be dreaming about?" I asked.

"I'm not sure. To be honest, I really don't know her that well. I've only been around her for a couple months. She kind of took me in when I had no place to go. It worked out…I ran errands and helped around her house."

"So where will you live now? Do you have family or friends in the area?"

"I live pretty much in this chair until they move her. I'm not sure after that."

"Can I help in any way? I mean, I don't want this to be weird in any way, but if there's something I can do to help you, I would be glad to."

Mary looked at me with the eyes of a young deer. Had she cried at that moment brown ink certainly would have stained her cheeks.

"That's very thoughtful of you, Matthew. I'll be fine."

It began to eat at me. I had a difficult time wrapping my head around the fact that Mary was soon to walk out of the hospital with no intended direction. I understood that a slice of our population, kids who are homeless and parentless, survive out there. But until now, they may as well have been refugees from foreign countries; they had never entered my circle. My only experience with any of them had been to drop a few bucks in their baskets.

I walked back to the cafeteria and bought two cups of coffee. I had paid attention to how Mary had fixed hers; three sugars and cream. I also withdrew two hundred dollars from the ATM in the hallway.

There were two visitors in Dad's room when I returned. A priest, Father Jimmy, was standing at the side of the bed. Maria, my ex-wife, sat in my chair.

I nodded as I crossed the room to deliver Mary's coffee. The Queen would not look away from Elaine.

"Nice of the two of you to stop by," I said. "Had I known you were coming I'd have brought extra coffees."

Maria smiled; the priest did not. He was carrying the black bag which contained all the gadgets associated with Last Rites. As an altar boy, I was familiar with, and terrified of, Extreme Unction, the sacrament that purifies the about-to-be-dead members of the Catholic Church.

The black bag brought it home for me. Had there been surgical instruments instead of candles and oil in it, I would have been no more hardened. My father was dying sooner rather than later. It was ordained.

He would be gone in a matter of days, I was sharing the room with a homeless girl I was suddenly and surprisingly in need of looking after, and the woman I had loved more than I had ever dreamed possible had infiltrated my defenses just when I needed them most. I needed to get out of there before I melted.

"Maria, please make sure you spend a few minutes with Dad before you leave. He's asked about you several times."

Maria was sitting on the edge of Dad's bed when I had gathered myself sufficiently to return. The Queen and Father Jimmy had gone.

My father had loved Maria and was devastated when we divorced. She had a terrific smile and an infectious laugh that would consistently make others in the room wonder what they had missed. She was a real beauty with black hair and dark eyes. She was the most appealing woman I had ever been around. Of course, there were the facts that a series of infidelities caused her marriage to crumble to dust and her husband to nearly drink himself to death, but Dad seemed almost able to look the other way with these. I never was completely certain he approved of the divorce, but I had resigned myself to its necessity on the grounds of self-preservation. I was also sure that my mother and protector Madeleine would have been supportive of my decision.

"George, you need to get better so that we can get out of here and catch up over a glass or two of wine," she said as she stood. She held Dad's hand in hers.

"Just as soon as I can, love," was his stock response.

I walked Maria to the elevator not sure whether to take her hand or push her down the shaft. I was silent for every step down the corridor. She used to tell me that if such an event existed, I would win a gold medal for silence.

"Who's the little girl?" she asked as we waited for elevator to reach our floor.

"She's related to that woman sharing dad's room. She's apparently very near death...they're taking her to a hospice soon."

"She's adorable."

And there it was. The parasite that infiltrated and infected every element of my relationship with Maria. She was incapable of trusting me, and eventually found no reason to act in a manner which would earn any faith in herself.

"Maria, my father is dying. Her grandmother is dying even faster. I bought her a fucking cup of coffee."

"Mattie. Mattie. It was just an observation. Chill a little bit, alright?"

"You're right," I said. "I'm just tired."

"With good reason. Listen, I have to run along, but please call me if I can be of any help. And get some sleep, Matt. You know how you get almost delusional when you're sleep deprived."

"I'm fine," I said, "it's the old man who's delusional now. He's convinced Madeleine's visiting him from the afterlife. And thanks for stopping by, Maria. It meant a lot to dad, I'm sure."

She kissed me on the cheek as the elevator door opened. Her lips may well have lingered a fraction of a second too long for the occasion, and they were clearly more moistened than I had anticipated.

"Billy," I said to his voicemail, "I need you to come down. Dad hasn't worsened dramatically; I just need to see you."

The instant I left the message I wanted it back. It was not the voice of a self-reliant man speaking. I pictured Bill frowning.

I wanted solitude and walked the hallways of the hospital for an hour.

Mary was curled in her chair when I came back, and she was crying. Instances wrapped in high emotion often put relationships on a faster track than normal. This seemed the case now, at least from my perspective. I'd known this girl for a matter of a day but was desperate to provide her some sense of calm, some degree of comfort. I worried about her living arrangements.

"Bad news?"

She appeared so vulnerable that to touch her shoulder would have caused her to melt into a different dimension. She swallowed and ran her fingers through her boy's haircut. Tufts of red pointed in many directions.

"They're moving her tonight or in the morning. She's going to die in a day."

"I want to say something that will help you, Mary, but I don't know what that would be. I want to do something for you, but I don't know what."

We sat in silence for ages. I revisited the day's emotional roller-coaster in my head as I sat watching the room darken. People can absorb anything if they have enough time to assimilate. I had been doing a decent job processing the fact that my father was dying. I had even surfed the tidal wave of emotion at seeing my ex-wife rather smoothly. But I was struggling with Mary's pain. She was such an odd combination of fragile child and appealing young woman that I had a hard time compartmentalizing my feelings. I didn't know who or what she was to me; I just knew that it was becoming all-encompassing. And I had met her yesterday.

"I'll be back shortly," I said to her. "Please tell my dad that I won't be long if he wakes up."

Dad was sleeping when I returned. It appeared Mary had not moved a muscle.

"You know, you've been sitting in that same position for almost 23 hours straight. Aren't you stiff as a board?"

"Yoga," she said.

"Has he been awake?"

"For about five minutes. He told me I looked pretty and then went right back out."

"You do look pretty."

"Glad to see all this hard work is paying off," she said.

I admit to seeing her more in the light of an attractive woman than a fragile child at that moment. She was very thin, that could be seen despite the baggy clothing. But she was a woman of 19 or so, and that brings a level of perfection, particularly to men ten to twenty years older.

"He's slipped today," I said returning to point. "I'm glad the Conqueror is showing up soon."

"The Conqueror?"

"My older brother William. He was a big-time athlete, has made a boatload of money. You know…William The Conqueror?"

"Where is he? This isn't something you should have to go through yourself. And I don't count the priest or the woman who were here earlier."

"Perceptive on your part. Bill owns a hunting and fishing lodge in Alaska. I left him a message to get here. He'll show up soon. I can count on him. What about you?"

She shook her head and exhaled loudly as she pulled the neck of her sweatshirt down. It was as if she needed to hold onto something for balance. The bottom of her throat was white and smooth.

"I have been avoiding thinking about that," she said.

I didn't rush.

"Have you eaten?"

She smiled openly for the first time I could remember.

"You caught me again. I took an apple off your dad's tray. He wasn't going to eat it."

We took the scenic route to the cafeteria this time, through the atrium in the center of the complex, and in through opposite doors. I remembered the suddenness of my mother's death. There had been no time to sort through emotions or expectations of grief. This demanded a different approach. I was sailing in uncharted waters, with Mary as my only companion and confident.

"You ever lost anyone?" I asked.

"Pets," she said. "I haven't seen my parents in a long time, but they're not dead. They don't approve of me, and I don't really care to be around them."

We sat in a cafeteria booth and ate nutritious and marginally tasty food. Mary's hunger finally trumped her uneasiness at allowing me to buy dinner. She ate like a deckhand on a big boat.

We pushed the two chairs close together when we got back to

the room. We didn't want our chatting to wake dad; at least that was the reasoning I decided to go with. For the nurses and other hospital workers, this was another Saturday night. For Mary and for me, this was as close to the end of the world as we were going to get.

We opened up to each other as perhaps only people suffering from genuine emotional exhaustion might. She told me about her estrangement from her parents, growing up on her own, living in self-determined poverty. I talked about my failed marriage, battling alcoholism and cooking.

I woke at three in the morning to catch a glimpse of the nurse exiting the room. Mary was half-way out of her chair and into mine. Her red head rested on my shoulder. She slept soundly despite the spinal contortion of occupying both chairs. Her hair smelled like wet earth; her breath was quiet.

I extricated myself without waking her, replacing my shoulder with a pillow. I covered her with the green blanket they had given her the night before and waited several seconds to make certain she was sleeping before leaving the room.

In the hallway, the light was down and there was no sound. I found a pen and paper at the nurse's station, and left Mary a note with my contact information. I hoped to be back before she and Elaine were gone, but I very badly wanted to shower and put on some clean clothes.

Just in case, I wrapped the note around the two hundred dollars I had withdrawn, and left it tucked into the brown and orange cloth bag that seemingly contained the entirety of Mary's belongings. Before leaving, I kissed the corner of her forehead more softly than I thought myself capable.

⌘

The first time my brother called our mother by her given name she laughed. That was all we needed to hear, and for the rest of her life we referred to her as Madeleine.

She was from a large and darkly Catholic family, and she passed down the mindset to her sons that God could as easily be found in an oak tree as a cathedral. I believed she feared priests more than respected them, and she did her absolute best to raise her sons outside the shadow of self-inflicted guilt under which all decent Catholics are apparently intended to live.

She was a bit of a brooder and could turn nasty on very short notice. She could forgive her husband's infidelities, but if she learned that someone had spoken badly about her potato salad, any chance of continued friendship would be dismantled.

Her first visits to me were in the aftermath of my divorce from Maria.

The divorce was difficult on me. Maria had been involved with another man, and my reaction upon finding out about it a year into the relationship was clinical. We made an effort. We went to counseling, had date nights, did some traveling. All this as I struggled with the images of my wife with someone else.

That kind of baggage, the inability to let it go, is death to any relationship, and ours was over in weeks. I have never fallen out of love with Maria, and I fully recognized from the outset that my emotional and mental peculiarities contributed to the end. After a couple trips to the hospital resulting from binge drinking, and after being told by my father to extricate my head from my ass, I eventually found a path of coping with my loss. Not so much fueled by forgiveness as much as a shrug.

Madeleine went quiet until my father's funeral.

Maria was dressed in black and wore a very tall and handsome man on her side. She had kissed my cheek and delivered a firm handshake to Bill as she entered the church. She and her companion sat quietly through the ceremony and departed before we all moved into the rectory for coffee and cookies. I didn't give her another thought until something woke me much later that night.

I had drowned the sorrow of burying my father and seeing the love of my life by knocking down a fifth of rum. I felt lousy and the kaleidoscopic dream images of Maria with an anonymous lover didn't help. I saw the bruises on the insides of her legs, her mouth red and slightly pulpy from being kissed too hard, the just-been-fucked hair the morning after she allegedly had fallen asleep at a friend's home.

"Don't forget the night she said she was ice-fishing with the guy at the restaurant."

This was Madeleine chipping in. The thought of Maria ice-fishing made Madeleine laugh. I drank a glass of water and tried to go back to sleep.

This became the process of my coping mechanism. I made it to work for a few more days after Bill departed, but I rather quickly reclaimed my frequent flyer status at the liquor store. After missing a week or so of work, I left my apartment only for necessities: alcohol and lunchmeat. Madeleine did her part by chronicling the events of Maria's behavior that should have told me that she was seeing another man. The old girl's visits were becoming more common and far less concerning. She didn't mind it that I had been hurt, she told me; what had really bothered her was that I had been made to look so foolish. About the only thing that kept her contributions to my self-sympathy becoming too bothersome was to drink. My rationalization was the loss of my father and a broken heart from a cheating wife. Madeleine certainly wasn't helping with all the reminders.

I sat on the porch of my apartment for hours each day wearing a cream-colored sweater my parents had bought me in Ireland. I often woke up stiff, sore and dampened from the dew at all hours of the night and early morning. My throat was sore from the weather and from throwing up each day.

Time was flying and nothing was moving at all in my world. It was a day or two later and I was awakened by a knock on my door. I had been napping on the sofa.

It was an office mate apparently sent by work to see what the hell had become of me. I spied him through the peephole. He knocked twice more before I cracked open the door.

"Jesus Christ, Matthew. Are you alright?"

"Not bad. Sorry to make you wait out there. I was napping."

"Hell, man, I don't want to intrude, but you and I have been friends for a lot of years. We've been trying to call and leave messages. We've e-mailed you. We want to make sure you're doing alright."

"I'm fine. Thank you for checking on me. I guess the death of my father threw me for a bit of a loop. I'll be back in the office in a day or two."

"Can I come in, Matthew?"

I remember opening the door and stepping to the side. The place was a wreck. I was somewhat aware that I had been drinking way too much, but the detritus of the last several days was alarming. Empty wine and liquor bottles were set up like bowling pins throughout the apartment. I had also resurrected my habit of smoking, and the stench of stale smoke added to the level of disgust my co-worker must most certainly have been experiencing. Madeleine was nowhere to be found.

"As you can see, the cleaning lady hasn't been around for a while. I'd invite you in to catch up, but I'll have to give you a rain check on that one."

He drank it all in in studied silence before answering.

"Listen, bud. I'm not going to get into your business, but you seem to have hit a really bad stretch here. You look like death, Matthew. Why don't you let me take you to see a doctor? We could hit one of those Minute Clinics and have you back here in an hour. I'm worried about you."

"You know what? I'm good," I said. "I just need to take a shower and get this place cleaned up. I'll probably see you at work in the morning."

"Tomorrow's Saturday, Matthew."

I watched him drive away from the roost of my porch. I went to the bathroom and took a look at the version of myself who had so worried my visitor. A bit scruffy, for sure, and in need of a shower and a shave. Thinner in the face, slightly jaundiced. Nothing a quick nap wouldn't fix.

When I woke, the Old Girl was reminding me that Maria had actually suggested a trial separation during our time of troubles.

"People, especially women, don't do that unless they have someone else in mind they want to be with," she was telling me. "She just wanted to be with someone else without the intrigue."

Madeleine was sitting in the dining area. I couldn't see her around the corner from my sofa, but her voice came through loud and clear.

"It's one thing to experience betrayal," she said, "God knows I suffered through enough of that with your father. But to have your nose rubbed in it…that's a different matter altogether. I would not have allowed myself to be played for a fool."

I walked to the kitchen and poured a glass of vodka. I grabbed a blanket from the sofa and went out to the porch, careful not to spill my drink.

A young woman beneath my perch was loading a little girl into a car seat in the back of her pale blue Honda. I may have noticed a wedding ring on her finger and wondered, I believe out loud, if she had ever fucked someone other than her husband.

I moved to the railing. The woman was directly beneath me as she emerged from securing her child.

"Excuse me," I heard myself saying with someone else's voice.

She looked up and smiled. Not an ounce of avarice.

"I just want to ask you to never betray your husband. It could kill him."

And I'm told that after imparting these words of wisdom on the sparkling young woman beneath me, I collapsed, hitting my head on the railing on the way down. I remember the ride in the ambulance; I have a hazy recollection of hospital workers asking me questions; I remember being moved from the emergency department into a room with a large window.

After waking and getting my bearings there in my hospital bed, I expected to see my father. I was alone until a doctor and nurse showed up an hour later.

"You're a very lucky man," the white coat was saying.

I heard words, but had difficulty stringing them together into coherence.

"Liver damage…poisoning…counseling…"

The noise faded as I dipped back into sleep. I dreamed of swimming in the ocean. I floated up and down on gentle waves of clear water. I tasted salt.

When I woke I felt pain for the first time. My body hurt. My cheek was sore and tight from the stitches needed to close the gash sustained in my fall. The room was dark and still.

Mary, the Queen of England, sat in the easy chair at the foot of my bed. Her legs were tucked up under her as she read from a book the title of which I could not make out. When she looked up and saw that I was awake, she smiled. I felt it as it floated its way to me on molecules of caring.

"I don't know if I'm dreaming, or if you're a ghost," I said, "but I'm very glad that you're here with me right now."

I started to cry. She smiled again, more fully this time, and went back to her book.

SAVING WOMEN

THE BUCKET LIST OF ITEMS to be experienced in 1970 by your typical testosterone-driven, athletic, handsome young man of twenty would, in all likelihood, not include grinding his way through seminary towards becoming a priest. Then again, none of those characteristics applied to John Dudley.

Dudley had entered the gate of St. Peter the Apostle Seminary two years earlier after two years of basic studies at a community college in Kalamazoo, Michigan. St. Peter's was located an hour north in the virulent enclave of Dutch Protestantism on Michigan's west coast. Its campus was small and tidy; its buildings were stone. Amenities were few, but the chapel seemed clearly to be the house of God with beautiful stained-glass all around.

Dudley's intention was to finish an under-graduate degree in Theological History while nibbling away at the coursework and priest stuff needed to be ordained. The workload didn't bother him. Nor did the fact that he was clearly missing out on the free sex, free thought movement that was sweeping over the country in 1970. The concept of sexual activity had remained in a dark corner of his brain throughout his young life. It was something he somewhat expected to come into the light eventually, but in the event it did not, he was not going to be disappointed. Free thought was an abstraction he could not wrap his brain around. By his thinking, all thought was free, so what the big deal was over this concept, he did not know or care about.

What prevented John Dudley from all but the rare smile was the future that lay before him. Becoming a priest had been a fallback plan to college and a regular job since his days as an altar boy back in

Kalamazoo. Now that he had taken steps toward the reality of this, he second-guessed himself to the point of a daily nervous stomach.

It was not a matter of faith. He had moved toward the light of the Almighty's grace as an over-weight twelve-year-old with bad skin as a means of mitigating the hurtful teasings of other boys, and he had stayed there. The jokes and jabs eventually became unbothersome as his deep belief in God washed the stings away. Dudley tossed and turned through sleepless nights uncertain whether or not he would be able to perform the non-religious tasks that would face him upon ordination. It was the job of priesthood that ate at him.

Seminary life was not terribly different from any life he had lived before. Dudley was a slightly lower-than-average student, and a merely adequate work ethic did not allow him to succeed easily. He was friendly to everyone but held only a couple of his fellow seminarians in what could be defined as friendship. He looked down often and when he smiled his eyes shut almost completely. He loved the absence of clothing choices the black uniforms provided.

Each Friday night after dinner he used the payphone on the wall in the hallway to call his mother. For a mother and son, they had very little to talk about. Dudley's father had been dead for several years, and there was no other immediate family to discuss. His mother Bernadette had a genuine interest in what all went in to the making of a priest, but her son's inability to relate any of this information with anything approaching enthusiasm kept the installments brief.

It was during a Friday call in late August that Dudley first expressed concern that the path he had chosen was not the right one.

"The real issue I'm facing is that I'm not sure what becoming a priest looks like. I mean, my feelings for God haven't changed. I believe that I've been called by Him to do something. More and more, though, I'm beginning to wonder if this is it. I look at these priests around here and they seem to have all the answers. I can pray with the best of them, I just don't know if I'm a person who can handle all the parish stuff. Once you're in, there are tons of responsibilities…tending the flock sort of thing. You have to be able to speak from a position of authority, and I don't think I can do that."

Bernadette Dudley, a strong-willed, liberal-minded woman of Irish stock took this bit of information in stride. She had watched her only child grow up through one failed endeavor after another and loved him not one tiny bit less. She had been excited when he brought up the idea of attending St. Peter's, but confidence that her boy had found a firm and final path to success did not overflow her cup.

"Maybe all you need is a little break," she said. "Talk to the head honcho and see if he'll grant you a pass for a couple weeks. You've been working very hard. Maybe you just need to recharge your batteries."

This tactic was out of her playbook: buy some time and perhaps the decision will be reconsidered. Not that she wanted her son to pursue a life plan that would not fulfill him. She simply wanted any decision he made to be carefully considered and allowed to develop over time. Snap decisions were not Dudley's strength.

The thought of sitting in Father Dulin's office and discussing such nebulous concepts as faith, God's plan and his own failure to embrace it made Dudley's stomach flutter and his hands instantly sweaty. He knew himself well enough to predict the outcome of that encounter.

"I don't know. Maybe I'll just stick it out."

"Nonsense," said his mother. "Now that you bring it up, I don't think there's one damn thing wrong with you asking for a little time off. How about this? I'm going north to spend a few days on Neebish with my aunt Bridge. She twisted her ankle and…well, to be honest, I just want to get up there and see her before it gets cold. Why don't you tell Father Muckity Muck that I need you to go with me? Tell him that you'll be gone for a week or so helping me take care of your aunt…your great aunt. Tell him that she lives on an island. And that she's blind. Have him call me in the morning."

Although Dudley failed to capture the moment for what it was, this was the newest installment in a series of instances where someone, usually his mother, took him off the hook. Had his mother not intervened just then, he'd have swallowed hard and stayed where he was until he'd had a nervous breakdown or took his vows.

"I am kind of on your way north, aren't I?"

He loaded his few belongings into the back of the giant, white Ford LTD station wagon his mother drove. He offered to drive, but she knew better. One, he had passed his driving test at the age of eighteen through Divine intervention, having almost thrown the poor DMV inspector through the windshield when a small dog ran into his path; two, he had never progressed beyond the new-to-driving stage of death-gripping the steering wheel at ten and two with his large and pudgy hands.

"I'll drive. You relax," she said.

They had a few hours and change straight north through rolling hills and a wide variety of evergreens, hardwoods and birch. She drove every foot of the way alert for coyote and deer and, further north, wolf and moose. Dudley molded himself into the passenger seat as relaxed and exhausted as a prison parolee. He slept and snored for a hundred miles but woke in time for a late lunch of cheeseburgers and fries.

"Do you remember the last time you were up here?" his mother asked as she eased the giant wagon on to the Mackinaw Bridge.

"I remember this bridge. It used to scare me something crazy when I was little. Five miles so high up over the water like this."

"Well, Aunt Bridge has certainly aged. I visited her last Summer. She's so frail now. Nothing to her."

"Why do you think she stays there?" asked the boy. "I remember it as being very remote."

"That's putting it mildly," said his mother. "And you can ask her why she lives there when you see her. She tells me to mind my own business."

The behemoth automobile developed a percussive rhythm as its wheels clicked over the steel grating of the bridge surface. John Dudley looked far to the horizon and avoided any glance at the water several hundred feet beneath them.

"Maybe I will," he said full to the brim in the knowledge that he would not.

The waters of the Great Lakes are working waters. There are islands and shorelines of splendid scenery, and thousands of tourists a year enjoy swimming, boating and fishing. But on balance these are waters that feed families. Giant ore boats a thousand feet long transport the mineral ingredients needed to produce steel; tons of wheat float from Canada's breadbasket provinces to markets around the world; though impacted by greed and disregard of natural resources, fish are still captured commercially for markets near and far.

For the most part, the people who lived in the towns and small cities along these shorelines were born there. Young people inherited trades and small businesses from their parents and grandparents. There was little need for infusion of new blood. If there had been, new blood candidates were not lining up. The weather ran to extremes; amenities were never abundant.

John Dudley knew all of this as a result of hundreds of question and answer sessions conducted during the car rides north as a boy. The drives were long, and there were just so many times a kid munching popcorn in the backseat could say the rosary as a distraction.

Neebish was a one mile by two mile rocky island in the tributary waters rushing between Superior and Huron. The big boats slid by on its southern shore through a channel dug deep and maintained by the Corps of Engineering people out of Detroit several hundred miles away. There seemed no reason for people to inhabit the place. The shorelines were rock more than sand, the water was cold as ice even in August and the ground was layered with relatively little topsoil.

"Tell me again how Bridge came to live up here?" asked Dudley as they inched further north towards the ferry dock that would connect them to Neebish.

"She was a spinster of sorts, probably in her thirties or early forties, never married, living with her parents somewhere near Saginaw. I think she had wanted to be a teacher. I'm not sure of the details, but she decided to marry an older man living on Neebish. Right out of the blue apparently. His people had settled there years earlier and actually tried to make a go of it with a fishing license. The man was a friend of Bridge's father, and she somehow started up a correspondence with him through the mail. It lasted a few months and off she went. She told me that the first time she saw anything more of a grainy photograph of him was the day she arrived for the wedding."

"That sounds courageous and a little crazy," said Dudley. "When did she lose her sight?"

"It was years after Hadlow…his name was Hadlow Egan…passed away. His health failed him very slowly. Cancer."

She stopped at the toll booth and handed the attendant a dollar.

"We all begged her to move closer to us. I mean, can you imagine living in that tiny cabin while you slowly lost your sight?"

Dudley let that sink in as he studied the landscape out his window. Prone to procrastination, he had never approached hardships or trouble with anything resembling enthusiasm or confidence.

"I'd be living in a nursing home in about ten minutes," he said without a hint of self-consciousness.

They made a quick stop for groceries in town before heading to the ferry dock. Provisions in hand, they drove the last miles of their journey through stands of birch and spruce. At the ferry dock, John Dudley got out and walked to the edge of the planking. A memory from his very early childhood…boys diving off the dock into the cold water…found its way back to him. Seven year-old John Dudley watching from the safety of the back seat of his parents' car in all-consuming amazement and awe.

The crossing took minutes, and the drive on gravel and rutted road to Bridge's place only minutes more. The mother wheeled the car into the sandy drive as if parking a horse-pulled hay wagon.

Dudley saw the door to the little cottage open and a woman of truly diminutive stature emerge. She held a cane. She smiled and waved in the direction of the behemoth car parked in her driveway.

Dudley and his mother grabbed the groceries and their travel bags and met her on the porch.

"Hello, Aunt Bridge. You're looking fit as a fiddle," said Dudley's mother as she dropped her bag and took her aunt's hands in her own.

The older woman gently placed her hands on her visitor's face. It was not a long process of recognition, and Dudley wondered if this method of greeting would be applied to his own face.

"Bern, you haven't changed a bit," said the old woman. "You didn't need to come all this way north simply to check on me but thank you for coming. It's nice having you here."

The old woman pointed toward Dudley without looking his way. "This the boy?"

"Hello, Aunt Bridget," said Dudley. "I'm John. I haven't seen you in a very long time."

"Come here," said Bridge. "And please don't call me Bridget. Call me Bridge like your mother does."

Dudley stepped toward her and was aware of his size. She was a small, thin woman who had never been large; he was tall and carried too much weight.

"May I touch your face?"

The courtesy of her asking for permission surprised him. How, he wondered, could anyone say no?

"You need to smile more," said Bridge as she traced her hands over his too-large cheeks and too-limited jaw line. "And maybe go just a little lighter on the pastries," she said with a smile.

Dudley felt blood rushing to his face as he forced himself to smile the criticism away. At this he excelled.

"Let's get unpacked," said his mother. "We have dinner to make."

They ate at the small table in the kitchen. Dudley felt like he was visiting a hobbit's house, too large for the surroundings and the furniture. He ate his pork chop slowly and went decidedly light on the boiled potatoes. He declined a piece of blueberry pie for dessert.

After washing up and playing several hands of rummy with Bridge's special cards, they decided in unison to turn in.

"I'm an early riser, you'll remember, Bern," said the aunt. "Everyone like coffee in the morning?"

Dudley curled his large body on to the couch in the living room. His length was greater than that of his sleeping quarter, but he made do. It had been a long day and he dozed off in ether comprised not slightly of guilt. It felt good to him to be so far away from St. Peter's.

He woke to as close to complete darkness as he had ever experienced. He lay listening to the clock tick. He could hear his mother snoring in the bedroom upstairs. Bridge's room was on the first floor through the opposite side of the kitchen. It was silent.

He was hungry and took this as a sin. Not a big sin for which God would dislike him, but a sin, nonetheless. He thought of the pie in the refrigerator. He would pray later for indulging in the snack that called out to him.

As quietly as a large man in a small dark room could probably be, he inched toward the kitchen. His first thought of not turning on the light made him smile.

"She's blind," he whispered to himself.

"Yes, she is," said his great aunt from the doorway to her room. "But she has bat senses and can detect movements in the dark. Turn on the light, John, and sit with me while you have some pie. And get a glass of milk to go with it."

"Talk to me about seminary," she said. "I had a cousin back in County Cork who was a priest. Not a very good priest by any account, but he looked good wearing the black."

"What happened?" asked the boy.

"I don't know the details…he's been gone a while, rest in peace… but it involved an indiscretion with a parishioner's daughter. They moved him to another parish like they do. So what's seminary like?"

"Well, I think it's probably a bit like being in the military. Everything we do, the classwork, the meetings, all of it seems to be focused very intently on preparing us for the job. Almost nothing we do serves any other purpose. To tell you the truth, it can get a little intimidating."

Bridge sat across the tiny table from her great nephew. Her fingertips gently touched the table as if playing a piano.

"I suppose every new thing we encounter can seem frightening," she said. "Do you have friends there? Other young men you can share your thoughts with?"

"A few. Many of the men there are not very priestlike. Some of them call me Father Dud."

In the moments of his life preceding this moment, John Dudley had learned to hide from and deflect unkindnesses rather than acknowledge their existences. When people or their actions stung him, his learned tendency was avoidance. The fact that he was sharing such a hurtful moment with the old woman, he could only assume, was due to the fact that she could not see him. It was confessing sins freely, secure in the darkness and ambiguity of the confessional closet.

"Well, you have to wash that off. Those men are smartasses, that's all. Tell me what's scary about it, John."

The boy sat quietly for a moment. He looked directly into Bridge's milky blue eyes, but only for an instant. He did not want to be caught staring in the event her vision returned.

"Once you're in, once you are ordained and sent to a parish someplace, you need to be able to handle the personal stuff. You're expected to be able to offer guidance and help with all of it."

"What stuff?"

"Saying mass, doing weddings and funerals and all of that is pretty straightforward. My Latin is improving, and most of the time we do those things in English anyway. The scary stuff, at least for me, is what the parishioners bring you. Their problems, their lack of faith, all of that. How am I supposed to know how to deal with these things when I haven't faced any of them myself? That's a lot of responsibility and I'm really not sure I'll be able to handle it."

Bridge drank this in. She played a one-hand solo on her invisible piano as her left hand moved to her lap.

"We used to have a wonderful priest here," she said. "We shared him with St. Joseph's over in town. There weren't enough priests for everyone to have one…even back in those days…and besides, we were such a small church that a part-timer was all we were ever going to get. Anyway, Father Savage…can you imagine a worse name for a priest?…was such a nice and thoughtful man. He visited me more often than he had time for while I was losing my sight. I always guessed that he had been an awkward boy growing up; he never seemed totally comfortable talking about real life issues. But he dealt with all of that. You might be able to, too."

Dudley finished the last swallow of milk.

"I pray for that," he said.

"He's been gone a long time," said Bridge. "A couple of the women from here on the island take me to the church once a month or so to sweep, get rid of the cobwebs. You should come with us, John. Walk around the old place. Maybe Father Savage will speak to you from the afterlife about being a priest. Maybe he'll send you some good vibes."

The next string of days were unaltered. Early morning coffee followed by an hour or so of local news on the radio. Bridge called the same two women at the same time each morning. The conversations were short and business-like. They were checking in. Very little discussion of family or personal experience was had.

Dudley was able to overhear planning for a trip to the church for the coming Saturday morning, and that news pleased him. He was not keen on meeting new people, but the possibility of dead priest vibes washing over him had a strong appeal.

In the afternoons, Bridge would sit in her ages-old easy chair and listen to two soap operas back-to-back on her television. She traced the letters of the alphabet with her right foot as therapy for her injured ankle. It was not swollen, and the skin was thin with a tinge of blue.

Dudley hiked for an hour each afternoon. His route along the waterline was rocky and the footing, at times, was challenging. The wind was always into him from the water, and he returned to the cottage with heavy breath and reddened cheeks. He slept soundly each night form-fitted on the couch that barely accommodated his frame.

After coffee Saturday he accompanied his mother and great aunt to the church. They were to meet the two other members of Bridge's troika and perform the monthly walk through. He had come around to looking forward to the visit. No misgivings.

St. Mark's was vintage north woods with tongue in groove flooring and cream colored plaster walls. The altar had not been rearranged so as to allow a priest saying mass to face his congregation. Upon noticing this, Dudley entertained the thought of how nice it would be to be able to perform this sacrament with his back to the herd. He would have been able to relax without all those eyes on him.

Unfinished wood shelving ran along both side walls, and accurately spaced statues rested in line upon it. Dudley inched slowly along each wall and inspected the saints. Several showed their age: a chipped sandal on Joseph; Mary's eroded finger. A plaque detailing the life and significance of each saint rested beside each statue.

Within minutes Bridge's two friends entered noisily. They moved to the front pew where Bridge was sitting, her cane resting across her lap.

"How's the ankle?" asked the taller and thinner of the women.

"Ankle's fine," said Bridge. "Do you two remember my niece Bernadette? Bern, this is Catherine and Electra."

As she identified the women, Bridge pointed accurately to the spot each of them stood. Radar. They were younger than Bridge, but they were not young.

"That's my great nephew inspecting the saints over there. John, come over here and meet these women."

Dudley shook each woman's hand with his sweating palm and returned to reading the wall.

"Well, let's get to it," said the tall and thin Electra. "I'll sweep and somebody else can dust the saints and the altar."

"What can I do?" asked the boy.

"Why don't you go in the sacristy," said Catherine. "Here's a dust rag. You can spruce the place up a bit. That's where father used to sit and prepare before he said mass."

Dudley entered the tiny room off the side of the church as if expecting to find a dead body. A small table that had been used as Father Savage's desk rested in front of the room's only window. Savage would have sat with his back to the light as he counseled his flock or wrote sermons.

A single shelf of books lined one of the walls. A variety of hymnals, their spines cracked and faded, took up most of the shelf space. A rustic wooden wardrobe of types took up most of the opposite wall. Savage's vestments for mass would have hung there.

Dudley stood at the shelving and took each book from its resting place. He gently caressed each with the dust rag before replacing it. He heard the women in the church talking, but this was background noise like whispers trying to reach us when we dream.

When finished with the bookshelf he wiped off the surface of the tiny desk. He walked around it through the sunlit particles of dust his cleaning had released and sat in the old priest's chair. Savage would have been a smaller man. Dudley moved the desk a few inches further away from the window to accommodate his larger wake.

He sat staring intently at the crucifix hanging over the doorway back into the church. It was modest, made of some hard and white plastic intended to portray marble. Age had given it a brown and yellow coloring.

"You'll have to ask him," came from the pews.

John Dudley opened the single drawer in the desk at which he sat. A tarnished and very thin medal rested among paper clips and short pencils. He had to read the tiny inscription to identify the saint as Christopher.

"Father, may I speak with you a minute?"

Tall and thin Electra stood in the doorway, her hands resting on each side of the door frame.

"Well, I'm not a priest yet," said Dudley, "so you really shouldn't call me father, but certainly you can speak with me."

His level of discomfort at having to speak to this stranger was intensified to an all but unbearable level at being trapped behind the tiny desk. He was certain that the warmth from the sun was magnified by the window behind him. There was no exit. He hoped he would not have a coughing fit, a common affliction when a room was overly warm.

Electra closed the door behind her and sat in the chair across the desk from Dudley. The boy sat in certainty that his heart was about to leave his chest. He could feel the beginnings of a sweat trail trickling down into the back of his shirt.

"Father Savage used to hear confessions in this room," said Electra. "He would put on his priest robes and sit sideways and listen to our sins before granting us absolution. I made a confession every week back then, and I miss doing so tremendously now. We just don't have any opportunity to do it. I wonder if you could do that for me now?"

She turned her chair to the side and stared at the bookshelf. Dudley turned his chair to the opposite wall the matter of inches that space allowed.

"You have to understand that I'm not able to…I'm not authorized to perform sacraments. I won't be ordained for at least another two years. This might actually be a sin in the eyes of God."

There was a moment of almost pleasant silence. The voices from the church were barely able to be heard; sounds of a bird's wings brushing the air.

Electra sat still and looked at the spines. Her mouth was slightly opened. She positioned a strand of gray hair behind her ear as she exhaled what had been a deep breath.

"Why don't you go ahead," he said. "We'll treat this like a conversation."

Without turning to him, Electra began.

"Bless me, father, for I have sinned. It's been many, many months since my last confession."

Dudley did not look at her as she presented her list of transgressions: uncharitable inclinations towards others, taking the Lord's name in vain, skipping mass even when it was available to her, impure thoughts while soaking in the bathtub, questioning the existence of a God that seemed to have abandoned her.

When she had finished, Dudley bowed his head and closed his eyes. His hands came together.

"I'm certain that if you pray for absolution, that God will grant it to you. I'm certain that if you reflect upon these sins and ask for forgiveness, it will be granted. These are not bad sins. You're here cleaning a church for goodness sake. I believe that what we need to do now is make a good Act of Contrition. After that, we'll both feel better."

When they had recited the prayer, when they had turned to each other and made eye contact, Electra exhaled once more.

"Thank you, father. I feel extraordinarily better."

"Again, I'm not a priest, but you're very welcome."

Dudley opened the desk drawer and removed the medal.

"Here," he said. "Please take this and keep it with you when you pray. It shouldn't be rusting away in this desk drawer when it could be doing you some good."

Electra took it in her palm and closed her long, thin fingers around it. When she rose and opened the door, fresh air, almost visible to John Dudley, poured in from the church.

THE GALAXY
LIMOUSINE COMPANY

PART ONE

A T TEN IN THE MORNING the first Monday of Morgan Arthur's retirement, she took delivery of a brilliantly yellow Porsche 911 turbo convertible. Never having driven anything but mainstream sedans and wagons, the car seemed out of place in her driveway. She had wanted something like this for ages but did not want to give anyone in her life the impression that she could afford it.

Morgan had just celebrated her sixtieth birthday and was eager to live a calmer life. She had spent fully half of her life in pharmaceutical sales and looked forward to the now countless opportunities to interact with people openly and honestly. Never an ass-kisser, the often borderline fawning over the grandness of intellect most doctors assumed to possess had grown more and more difficult to pull off the closer to the end of her career she came. She could now tell it like it was. And she could now drive her manual transmission, zero to sixty in the bat-of-an-eye car pretty much wherever she wanted to.

Where she did drive on the maiden voyage was to the two-room, dull and shabby office of the City of Roanoke Women's Aid Society to begin the first two of her eight hours of orientation and training. This was required prep work for all volunteers. Yolanda, the very large woman orchestrating the session, explained that the eight hours would be covered over three days. Volunteers as a group did not maintain a high degree of focus after a couple hours, she explained. She also, by way of introduction, shared with Morgan that she had been a battered wife before earning multiple degrees in Social Work and making this her life's work. Morgan took copious notes, was a fully-engaged, active listener and waited for the bell to ring. The car called to her throughout.

"We're so glad to have you join us," said Yolanda at the end of the first session. "This can be a very stressful volunteer gig. Not to scare you off, but some of the situations you'll be involved in might be pretty intense. We certainly need all the help we can get."

"Listen," said Morgan as she shook Yolanda's hand with a firm grip, "I just spent the last few years of my life coming to terms with the fact that I made a living selling opioids, along with other drugs of course. My husband passed away six months ago, and that's been rough. He was one of those guys who took care of everything…all the minutia of owning a house and cars, money, everything. I can handle stress, trust me."

In the months since her husband's death Morgan mulled over the thought of relocating. Roanoke, Virginia had been their home since marriage. It was a medium-sized city that offered precisely what Morgan and her husband had wanted: a couple of good restaurants, low crime and a convenient airport.

The house was too large for her, but only slightly. She had struggled with the catharsis of removing all of her husband's clothes, but pictures remained on walls and books on shelves to remind her of her loss. She cried less often, but with the same intensity of grief as the day he died.

The volunteer work, she was sure, would help her. Working with youth was an option she quickly opted against. She had decided at quite an early phase of adulthood that she did not want children and had married a man of the same thinking. She considered hospice work but knew that this would open again and again the wound her husband's death had left.

Young women in need of support and guidance seemed the path best suited to her. She had spent her career in a male-dominated world and had come to grips with the frustration of so few options to deal with slights, professional and personal. Morgan had never been physically mistreated by a man, but thought she understood the oppression that came with being stuck in a situation with no choices to get out. She allowed herself to feel a bit excited the day she finished her volunteer training, and she looked forward to her first case.

"If you're ready to get started, I have someone in mind that seems like a good fit for you."

This was Yolanda bringing Morgan up to speed as they ate salads for lunch at an outdoor café in town. It was a warm March afternoon, and Morgan enjoyed the sunshine. In another couple months it would be too hot and humid to sit outside. Central Virginia experienced all four seasons, but summers were the real standouts.

"Tell me," said Morgan.

"Her name is Amber, and she has two children...both girls...ages six and four. Not married, but the father of the girls has been a real issue. Kind of standard fare: he accused her of having an affair, two instances of domestic violence, one trip to the hospital. She's living at the shelter now with the kids. There's a personal protection order in place, but she needs some coaching as to effective steps to move on to the next level. She has no formal education after her junior year in high school. Very low on the worldly sophistication meter."

Morgan processed the scenario and began to catalogue a list of action items that she would need to walk Amber through.

"Has she worked?"

Yolanda had just taken a large bite of breadstick and held up one finger requesting a moment to chew and swallow.

"She has. Clerk jobs at a grocery store and, I think, Walmart. That appeared to be the trigger. She had no money, and when she made an effort to get some, the ex suspected her of infidelity. This is really common, by the way."

"Sign me up," said Morgan. "What's our next step?"

"Wonderful. You're going to do her a world of good. I dare say she's never had a positive role model of any kind, let alone a woman. I'll set up a meeting in my office so we can all get acquainted. Tomorrow work?"

"Tomorrow's perfect. Pick a time and I'll be there."

There was a voice mail waiting for her when she returned home. Following lunch with Yolanda, she had taken an hour-long drive along the Blue Ridge Parkway. Although the speed limit was a boring 25 miles an hour, she did her best to channel a Formula One driver as she shifted gears and negotiated the sharp curves.

"Morgan, it's Eddie Rembrandt down at the office. Hope you're doing well. I really feel like crap that I haven't reached out to you since Elliot's funeral. Anyway, a package arrived for Elliot, so if you could call me back, I'll work out someway to get it to you. Again, I hope you are doing OK."

She took a moment to pour a glass of wine before returning the call to her late husband's office.

"Eddie, Morgan Arthur."

"Hey, Morgan. Thanks for calling me back. As I said, a package showed up today for Elliot. It was marked personal, so obviously I didn't want to open it. Would you like me to have someone bring it by the house?"

"No, I have to do some stuff in town tomorrow anyway, so I'll just swing by the office, if that works. It would actually be nice to see some of you."

"It'll be great to see you, too. How are you doing? How are you holding up?"

"About as well as can be expected," she said. "Nothing really prepares us for this, right? I'm staying busy and trying to look forward. Oh, I bought a new car."

"What did you get?"

"I'll show you in the morning. Thanks for calling me, Eddie. See you tomorrow."

The next morning was sunny and breezy. She took a two-lane back road as a detour into town. The more capable a driver she became, the more she enjoyed the immediate acceleration her car offered her. It took her several days before she cracked eighty, but it was nothing to hit a hundred now. She kept a sharp eye open for animals and speed traps.

Morgan pulled into the lot and parked in a visitor slot. Her husband had climbed to the upper edge of middle management at an insurance agency, and this had been his home away from home for the last several years of his life. The agency was family-owned, and he had been highly-respected and treated extremely well.

It was an odd sensation that flowed over her as she entered the reception area. The world skipped a beat in its rotation; her husband would not be walking out to greet her and take her to lunch.

The receptionist buzzed Eddie, and within a matter of seconds he was shaking her hand and leading her back to his office. It was a cold consolation that the door to her dead husband's office was closed, the new occupant apparently on the phone.

She sat across from Eddie and scanned the credenza behind him.

"How's the family?"

"Everyone is doing well, thanks. The kids are involved in everything. Marlene doesn't get a minute's rest."

Morgan nodded.

"Please tell her I asked about her."

"I sure will," said Eddie. "I'm sure she'll call you. Maybe meet for lunch."

They both sat in the uncomfortable silence the knowledge that no such phone call and no such lunch would ever transpire.

"Well, here you go," said Eddie handing a package about the size of a shoebox across the desk. "It arrived a couple days ago."

"Well, won't this be exciting?" she said as she placed the package in her lap. "If it's anything to do with work, I'll be sure and let you know."

She looked again at the photos behind Eddie. Happy family. Well trained dog.

"Eddie, thank you so much for contacting me. I won't keep you, but please tell Marlene to give me a call sometime."

They shook hands before joining in a perfunctory hug.

"Oh, what kind of car did you get?" he asked.

"Walk me out. You'll want to see it."

She sat in the lot and opened the package. A bottle of high end champagne and a hand-written note.

Elliot,

Just my annual gift to thank you for your help all those years ago. I'd never have had a chance without you.

Patrick

The note was written on business letter head: The Galaxy Limousine Company. The address was in a warehouse section out near the airport, so she decided to merge into the fast lane and check it out. She was not due to be at the women's shelter for another hour, so she welcomed the distraction.

The address was situated at the end of a dead-end street named Industrial Boulevard. It was a massive warehouse with no landscaping and zero interest in looking anything other than what it was. Several limousines, white and black and of varying passenger capacity, were parked in the lot in front along with a black Cadillac SUV that appeared to be brand new. A large garage door was open; a walk-in door with a sign declaring it to be the office was just to the left and closed.

Morgan slowed to a crawl as she neared the driveway. It would be simpler and less worrisome to simply call the phone number on the note's letterhead. But this was a mini-adventure. She would be meeting a woman in need of strength and structure in an hour or so, and the thought of anything other than a face-to-face with the gift-giver was simply and quickly ruled out. She needed to be intrepid. Her curiosity meter was in the red.

She parked the Porsche and walked in the garage door. There were two rather large men in dress slacks and sleeveless undershirts sitting on folding chairs next to a limo. The hood of the vehicle was up, and she guessed that they had been working on it. Both men were smoking cigarettes and spoke in what Morgan presumed was Russian.

"Can I help you?" said the larger of the men in a pronounced accent.

"Yes, thank you," said Morgan. "I'm looking for someone named Patrick. I'm sorry, I don't know his last name."

There was ten seconds of uncomfortable silence before the large man stood and approached Morgan. He was easily six and half feet tall and had very broad shoulders. He had long, slightly dirty hair pulled back in a pony tail. His cigarette dangled from his lower lip as he wiped his hands with a handkerchief. His eyes were intensely blue, and he stared at her without blinking.

"I'll see if he's here. Your name please?"

"Morgan Arthur. My husband's name was Elliot Arthur. I believe he and Patrick were acquaintances."

The large man smirked slightly as he walked toward the warehouse office. He knocked once at the office door and left her.

Morgan looked around and catalogued the large building: folding chairs, a couple of desks in opposite corners. No artwork or posters on the walls, and the windows were painted.

"You like a cigarette?" the other Russian was asking.

"Thank you, no," she said. "So how many limousines do you have?"

"Most are at home with drivers. These here are...fucked up."

"I see."

She was relieved when the larger Russian returned from the office.

"He'll be right out. You want a cigarette?"

Morgan smiled at the other man. Before she could answer, the office door opened and a man she did not recognize emerged.

Patrick Blount was as large as the big Russian. He wore a dark suit with white socks and black Oxford dress shoes. His white shirt was starched and neatly pressed. He smiled with perfect teeth as he extended his hand. Morgan was immediately aware of her hand disappearing almost completely in the huge, but gentle handshake. She also took notice of the impressive scar along the left cheekbone of the man greeting her.

"Mrs. Arthur. What an absolute pleasure meeting you. Believe it or not, I've heard a lot about you. Your husband and I are friends."

"Thank you," she said. "I'm sorry, but you apparently don't know that Elliot passed away some time ago. It was very unexpected. A heart attack."

Patrick Blount added his left hand to the greeting. He shook his head.

"I am so sorry," he said. "Elliot and I have known each other for years. I feel awful that we did not keep up more recently. I'm so sorry for your loss. He was a truly good man."

He released her hand and motioned to the office door.

"Please, won't you come in and chat for a bit?"

This last statement reached Morgan's ear with a slight accent she would have guessed to be Appalachian.

"Thank you, but only for a moment," she said. "I have an appointment shortly back in town."

The office was as decorated and as tidy as the warehouse was not. In addition to several photos of a small dog…some sort of terrier…there were pictures of wrestlers all around the place.

Patrick sat behind the desk and motioned Morgan to one of the chairs facing him.

"I'm sorry, but I have to ask," she said, "what's with all the pictures of the wrestlers?"

He smiled another perfect smile.

"It's me. Well, it was me. I used to wrestle professionally. Not big stuff on TV, although I did appear on a couple shows. Mostly barnstorming events that traveled through the south. I was the designated loser. That was a long time ago."

"I find that simply fascinating," she said. "So how did you get into the limousine business?"

"That's where your husband came in. Would you like a bottle of water, Mrs. Arthur?"

"No thank you, and please call me Morgan."

Patrick rose and walked to a refrigerator in the corner of the room. He returned to his desk with two bottles.

"Just in case you change your mind."

"And this is your dog?" said Morgan pointing to a photo on the desk.

"That's my baby. I spoil her something rotten."

Morgan sat comfortably and listened to the very large man tell her how he and her husband had met. She accepted the water after his third offer.

"I wanted to start this company," he told her, "but nobody would do business with me. I had done my homework, had a business plan all in place, the whole nine yards. But in those days…this was eleven years ago…people just didn't want to do business with people like me."

"Wrestlers?" she asked.

"Gays," he said. "Well, and I had a little trouble with the law after my career ended. I did a little time. I guess bankers don't like that either."

She sipped at her water and sat with her mouth open. Elliot Arthur was a mid-level manager of an insurance company. Not what anyone would call a physical man by any means, he had been a loyal and devoted husband.

"How in the world did you connect with Elliot?"

"I was kind of bouncing from job to job, and my boyfriend got me a part time gig at a lounge he was waiting tables and bar-tending at. I bussed tables, did some bouncing, whatever they needed. Anyway, Elliot would stop by after work once in a while...he was not big drinker, I can tell you that...and he got to know Drew, that was my boyfriend's name. They got to talking a little about me, and it worked out that I met up with Elliot."

"And Elliot helped you get started in your limousine business?"

"Yes, and I will forever be thankful. He loaned me enough money to put a down payment on a couple vehicles and the rest is history. Even though I paid him back on time...a little early actually...I send him a bottle of champagne each year just so he knows how life-changing his help was."

"Wow. I never would have guessed," said Morgan. "The things we don't know about people in our lives, right? So you appear to be doing well with the business?"

"I pay the bills. We have a solid repeat customer base. We've expanded a little bit outside of giving people rides...running errands and making deliveries, some collection stuff...tasks that are a bit out of the mainstream. There's good money in that. Anyway, none of this would have been possible without your husband's help."

Morgan placed her empty water bottle on Patrick's desk.

"Well, Patrick, I've taken up enough of your time and I really need to be going. It was a pleasure, and a real education to talk to you."

His face stiffened. He adjusted the position of a tape dispenser on his desk-top.

"There is one more thing," he said.

Morgan picked up her empty water bottle and twisted the screw top back and forth.

"I told Elliot, early on, that if there was ever anything he needed...anything at all...that I was a phone call away. That I owed him that. I'm not talking about nefarious activity here. Just that if he needed help in an area he wasn't comfortable in, that it would be taken of and he would never have to be concerned about it. I'm making that same commitment to you, Morgan. A phone call. Kind of a get out of jail free card."

"That's quite an offer, Patrick. I'll certainly call you if I ever need you."

They rose and exited the building through the door to the parking lot. Patrick walked her to her car and opened the driver-side door.

"Nice ride," he said.

"Thanks. I'm developing a case of delayed buyer's remorse, actually."

"Let me know if you want to move it," said Patrick. "I know some people who could get you top dollar for it."

Morgan slid in and started the engine. Patrick gently closed her door.

"Patrick, may I ask you one more thing?"

"Anything, Morgan."

"What was the name of the lounge?"

He nodded and smiled with closed lips.

"Cowboy Billy's," he said. "It had a distinctive clientele in those days."

"Patrick, was my husband gay?"

"I really don't think so, Morgan. I never saw anything that would lead me to think that. I'll tell you what. I think he just liked the company."

Her first meeting with the woman at the Aid Society was immediately less an event on her horizon than before she had met Patrick Blount. Her mind raced at high speed as she drove the Porsche towards town. This was a ton of information to process, and Morgan wanted to sit in her kitchen and drink a few glasses of wine. She parked on the road in front of the shabby office. The box containing the bottle of champagne went into the trunk.

Yolanda sat at her desk and greeted Morgan as she entered. A very slight and seemingly very shy woman sat opposite her. The young woman had straw colored, straight, shoulder-length hair which she parted in the middle. Her hands were placed in prayer on her lap.

"Morgan, so good to see you again. Please come over and meet Amber Dix. We've just been talking about you."

Morgan walked to the desk and extended her hand to Amber. The handshake, she noticed, was weak and a bit clammy.

"Very nice to meet you, Amber," she said, "I very much look forward to working with you."

"Thank you, ma'am," said the young woman with a throat that needed clearing.

"No, right off the bat, let's be clear about something," said Morgan. "I am Morgan, not ma'am. Sound good?"

The woman smiled and nodded. Eye contact, although not a full second in duration, was established between the two women.

After the introductory session with Yolanda, Morgan drove her new friend to the Women's Shelter. The shelter was located in a non-descript neighborhood several miles away. Morgan took the scenic route; she was not as concerned about being followed to the somewhat secret location as much as she wanted more time to talk with Amber.

"This is a really nice car," said the young woman. Her accent was pure Tide commercial. Her eyes, light blue, captured the sunlight.

"Thank you. I probably need my head examined for getting it. I'm not sure I'm going to keep it, but it is certainly fun to drive."

"I bet," said Amber.

"You have a driver's license, Amber?"

"I had one, but it expired. I got it when I turned sixteen, but my ex...well, he didn't like me having it. We only had one car, anyway."

"Well, that's certainly something we probably want to put on our list of action items, isn't it? A car might be down the road a little for you, but you should have a license, if for no other reason than to have formal identification."

"I would like that," said Amber.

Morgan flashed her new Aid Society volunteer badge to the woman checking in visitors and followed Amber through the kitchen toward the bedroom where the young woman and her children slept. The kids were playing in a fenced-in backyard, and Amber waved to them from the sink window.

"They're my life," she said. "I'm so happy this place exists so that we can be here."

The bedroom was tiny and barely had floor space for the two twin beds. The nightstand between the two beds held an alarm clock and a photo of an older woman standing in front of a brown-colored house trailer.

"Who's this?" asked Morgan.

"That's my momma. She's dead now. She barely knew the girls, but I want them to know that she's still in their life. I want her remembered by the girls."

"That's nice. I think the connection is important."

They sat on the twin beds and faced each other. Morgan had brought a notepad and pen along. She sat with her legs crossed and took notes as they spoke. Amber sat with her knees together and her spine as straight as a tall tree.

The list they developed over the next thirty minutes seemed daunting to Amber. She had spent the last several years of her life purposely avoiding any activity outside of the repetitive existence in which she lived. Now she was helping to create a list of action items that both thrilled and frightened her.

"OK," said Morgan as she scanned her notes, "driver's license, school and day care for the girls…we can ask about community aid for that, a job…really any kind of job just to get you established. We'll start snooping for an apartment that's within bus or walking distance for you and the girls. How are the girls set up for clothes?"

When no answer had been offered, Morgan looked up across the ravine separating the beds. Amber's head was bent down and rested in her hands. Very quietly and very gently she wept.

Morgan moved to sit beside her and put an arm around her shoulder.

"It's a lot to process, Amber. I get that. But you need to know that I will be with you every step of the way. We'll get there together."

The young woman sniffed and wiped her nose with the back of her hand.

"I'm not overwhelmed, Morgan. Really, I'm not. I've been waiting for a chance to do this. To be safe and not scared to death. To be able to show my daughters how women are supposed to act. I'm not overwhelmed. I'm thankful."

"You'll do great," said Morgan.

"It is all kind of moving fast though, isn't it?" said Amber Dix.

"I drive a Porsche. What do you expect?"

In the days that followed, the two women attacked the list as if planning an invasion of a small country. Morgan prioritized so that as each task was completed, the flow of the master plan made chronological sense. Amber injected an enthusiasm and positivity that Morgan had rarely seen. They spoke often of the future.

Looming like a funnel cloud out on the horizon was Amber's court date with the father of her children. Custody was pretty much signed, sealed and delivered; family court judges paid close attention to past instances of physical abuse. Amber's attorney, a young and very underweight woman fresh out of law school, had procured the necessary police and hospital records intended to sway the judge's opinion.

"This is no doubt going to be a slam dunk," she said as Amber and Morgan sat in her firm's conference room.

Morgan sat quietly and observed. Amber had come a great distance since they met. She made eye contact when speaking; she smiled regularly, but not now.

"I'm not so concerned about what the judge is going to say," said Amber. "When I think of being there in the same room as Cody, my stomach flips."

"We'll be there with you," said Sara the attorney. "You have nothing to worry about."

"You have no idea," said Amber.

Morgan noticed a patch of red blotchy skin developing on Amber's neck, as if the young woman's new-found confidence were attempting to leave through her pores. Amber's breathing had also gone from steady-as-a-scuba-diver to hurried and short.

"Sara," said Morgan, "why don't you walk Amber through the proceeding. What it'll look like. What she should expect from start to finish."

"That helped," said Amber as they drove toward the Women's Home. "It helped that I have an idea what to expect. Cody's just so intolerant sometimes. He just flies into a rage at the slightest thing. I know he's going to lose his shit."

"Well, the judge has probably seen all of it before a million times. You're strong. His nonsense is beneath you now. You don't need to let it affect you."

"I'll just be glad when the whole thing's over."

Two weeks before the court appearance, Amber started working the evening shift as a barista at a Starbucks. She walked a half mile from the Women's Home to a bus stop and rode fifteen minutes to work. The girls were well cared for at the home, and Amber, really for the first time in her adult life, was able to move through her day awash in optimism and good thoughts. Her hair was always pulled back and her black slacks were always pressed.

She enjoyed the camaraderie that quickly developed with her fellow workers. Although determined not to seek out or accept any attention from men for a long time, it was a new experience to be able to chat openly without looking over her shoulder for Cody.

She met with Morgan two or three times a week. The introverted and shell-shocked woman she had been when they first met had morphed into almost effervescence. In Morgan's weekly reporting to Yolanda, she laid out the time-table.

"She'll have enough money saved to get an apartment in a few weeks," said Morgan. "I know that it goes against protocol, but I might help her out a little."

"We don't ask that of our volunteers," said Yolanda, "but I know how close the two of you have become. I'll tell you, Morgan, this is one of the real success stories of the year for us. You've done a terrific job."

"We just needed to get her pointed in the right direction. She's done the rest."

Morgan dressed for court as if she were going on a sales call. It had been a while since she felt inclined to impress anyone, but this was certainly one of those occasions. She wanted desperately for Amber to project professionalism and independence; dressing the part herself could only help.

Amber looked like a suburban housewife as she walked down the drive to Morgan's car. They had shopped together earlier in the week for the dark green dress and cream colored sweater. As the two women wore the same size shoes, Amber had selected a very pricey pair of flats.

"You doing okay?" asked Morgan.

"I really think I am," said Amber sliding into the car and fastening her seat belt. She exhaled a large breath. "Let's get this shit over with, shall we?"

Morgan smiled broadly as she slipped the car into gear.

Sara the attorney met them in the hallway outside the courtroom. She appeared slightly less assured of herself than when they had met in the conference room, but did her best to exude as much confidence as possible.

The proceedings went as expected. Morgan sat in the gallery and stared at the back of Cody's head. It surprised her that he did not speak, deferring to his attorney at every opportunity. It also surprised her that he was a rather unprepossessing guy. She would not have guessed him to weigh 160 pounds.

When called upon, Amber answered with a strong and clear voice. The responses she and Sara the attorney had practiced were unadorned and to the point. Custody of her children was awarded to her; supervised visitation for the father was established; child support payments were mandated.

"Your honor," said Sara as they were nearing the end of the proceedings, "may we request that the protection order currently in place remains in effect?"

"Granted," said the judge. To Cody's attorney he said: "you can request for this to be revisited in six months."

Sara, Amber and Morgan lingered in the courtroom until everyone had gone. Despite great effort, and in violation of the promise she had made to herself, Amber placed her head on Morgan's shoulder and cried.

The phone jangled her awake at two in the morning. She had finally opened the bottle of champagne sent to her husband as a bit of a victory celebration and was groggier than normal as she answered.

It was Yolanda, and the words that rode the phone lines to Morgan's ear were chopped.

"Amber…on the way home from work…attacked…beaten…hospital."

Morgan showered and dressed in jeans, a sweater and pair of running shoes. She drove the speed limit to the hospital and walked silent as a Ninja down the hallway to the intensive care ward.

Amber's face was puffy and red. A cut on her left cheekbone had been closed with stitches. Her lips were swollen and her eyes bloodshot.

The young woman opened her eyes when Morgan took her hand. "Did Cody do this to you?"

"I can't do this," said Amber. "I can't do this, or he'll kill me and the girls."

PART TWO

When the police visited Amber at her new apartment two weeks later, she had nothing to tell them. She had not been aware that Cody was a no-show at work, that his apartment had by all accounts been abandoned, and that his car remained in the lot at the complex.

She was able to share with them that she had not seen Cody since their court date. She also stressed that she had no idea as to the identity of whoever had attacked her that night. These last two statements were lies of course but lies that she felt comfortable telling.

In reality, Amber had no way of knowing any of the details. She could not have known that following a night of heavy drinking, and after dangerously driving himself home, the father of her children had entered his dark and dingy apartment to find two surprisingly well-dressed men speaking Russian. Amber could not have known that the Russians carried an unconscious Cody down a flight of stairs and placed him rather ungently in the trunk of a black town car. And she certainly would have had no knowledge that the Russians then drove several hundred miles through the night before shooting their prisoner twice in the back of the head and depositing his lifeless body in a shallow grave they dug wearing expensive shoes. Cody had pissed himself while riding in the trunk along the way, but a quick stop at a self-car wash on the way back to Roanoke had taken care of that. She could not have known this either.

When Patrick Blount opened the box the UPS man had just delivered, he smiled with those perfect teeth. He placed the bottle of champagne on the window ledge behind his chair. He would need a special occasion to open it.

Printed in the United States
By Bookmasters